CW00544760

CURSED COCKTAILS

S.L. ROWLAND

AETHERVALE
PUBLISHING

ALSO BY S.L. ROWLAND

Cursed Cocktails Copyright © 2023 by S.L. Rowland

SLRowland.com

Cover design by Lucian Acatrinei

Map by Cartographybird Maps

All Rights Reserved. This book may not be reproduced or used in any manner without the permission of the author.

This is a work of fiction. Names, characters, places, and incidents either are the products of the author's imagination or are used fictitiously. Any resemblance to actual persons, living or dead, businesses, companies, events, or locales is entirely coincidental.

ISBN 979-8-9878502-0-6 (Paperback)

ISBN 979-8-9878502-1-3 (Hardback)

Published by Aethervale Publishing

❀ Created with Vellum

For anyone who has ever wished for a chance to start over.

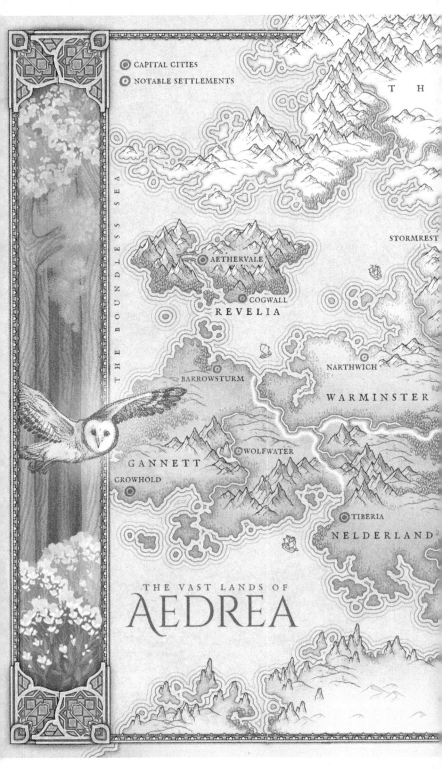

CAPITAL CITIES
NOTABLE SETTLEMENTS

T H

STORMREST

AETHERVALE

COGWALL

REVELIA

NARTHWICH

BARROWSTURM

WARMINSTER

GANNETT

WOLFWATER

CROWHOLD

TIBERIA

NELDERLAND

THE VAST LANDS OF
AEDREA

PROLOGUE

Thick snowflakes drifted through the air, concealing the sprawling wilderness of the frozen north. Rhoren scanned the area to no avail. A storm like this concealed everything.

He called on his blood magic, and his veins screamed. Heartbeats suddenly pulsed around him like rolling thunder. To his left and right, the hearts of dwarves and men beat rapidly, almost frantically—a testament to the danger they faced. Fifty yards to the west, a den of direfoxes throbbed slowly as they slept beneath a snow bluff. Even in frigid climates like this, life endured.

Rhoren tuned out the noise, searching for an unmistakable beat among the chaos. The scouts had spotted a behemoth moving south. The monsters moved faster than anything their size had a right to, and their armored scales made them almost unkillable. If they didn't stop it now, he knew all too well the havoc it could wreak.

The blood mage focused, blocking out the pain as he spread his blood sense outward in all directions. The anarchy of life multiplied, a turbulent ocean of beating hearts, and then he heard it—the thunderous pounding of the behemoth's heart.

He let his magic fade and the relief was euphoric, if only for a few passing moments. Rhoren signaled in the direction of the behemoth, ignoring the uncontrollable gulp of Jaren, his second-in-command, as they moved in silent pursuit.

The soldiers were useless against a monster of this magnitude, and they all knew it. A hundred of them would die before they even pierced the beast's skin. Their job was to protect Rhoren while he danced with the devil, and if the unfortunate happened, to carry his body back to camp.

Rhoren steeled himself and set off toward the monster with soldiers flanking him on both sides. Archers brought up the rear. He massaged his knuckles, thankful for the bite of the cold to ease some of the burn. After almost twenty years of service, the ache never truly faded. He would be paying for this day for weeks.

A tree snapped in the distance, and a crow darted across the white sky. They were close.

He held up his hand, his charcoal skin a beacon against the whiteness as he signaled for his men to stand back.

Twenty paces out, a blur of gray moved through the snow before disappearing. Rhoren readied himself. He was too close to use his blood sense now. If caught unaware, there'd be no time for an offensive attack.

Blood magic was a delicate balance. The magic was powered by his own body, and each spell took its toll. Too little and it might not be effective; too much and he could overburden himself. Every battle was a tightrope walk. With a behemoth, he was walking on a razor's edge.

But with less than a dozen blood mages in the entire nine kingdoms, Rhoren couldn't turn his back on the realm.

A loud roar echoed behind him, and he turned just in time to watch the behemoth hit one of the archers with enough force that he flew through the air, body crumpling in the snow as he landed. The behemoth roared, and snow fell from nearby trees.

Soldiers held their swords at the ready against the monstrous beast. It took bravery to join the Northern Guard, and his men did not disappoint. They would die if they needed to, but Rhoren would do everything in his power to prevent that.

The behemoth stood on two legs, easily twelve feet tall as it towered over his men. The creature resembled a bear, if that bear were covered in impenetrable, magically-resistant armor. Thick, diamond-shaped scales, each one the size of a hand, protected the monster in all areas. They could be pried off with enough force, but no one who had attempted the act on a living behemoth had survived to tell the tale.

Some said that the scales of a behemoth rivaled a dragon's. Rhoren believed it.

Jaren unleashed a battle-cry as he charged the monster. Any other time, it might have rallied the others, but when the behemoth answered with a cry of its own, it was like a pup next to a wolf. Spittle flew from the beast's mouth as its jaws spread wide, revealing the two piercing saber-teeth that could bleed a man out in minutes.

The behemoth swiped, and Rhoren countered. His

entire body burned as he froze the monster in place. The action exerted so much effort that he couldn't even yell for Jaren to move. Luckily, the man took notice and retreated to the others.

Sweat beaded down Rhoren's face, matting his black hair to his brow as he released his hold over the monster.

Arrows clattered off the behemoth's scales as the archers aimed for its eyes. Rhoren cursed. They knew better, but somehow being face-to-face with death made even the most battle-hardened soldiers lose their senses.

"Retreat!" Rhoren shouted. He needed to end this soon.

The behemoth set off in pursuit as his men obeyed. The time was now or never. He wiped his brow and prepared for a world of hurt. Rhoren's vision darkened, and the enormous heart of the behemoth pulsed within his mind. His neck seized and knees threatened to buckle as the monster's core buzzed with energy that called to the blood mage. Rhoren cradled the behemoth's heart with his magic and squeezed. There was a distant roar, but it was nothing compared to the scream of his own veins. His joints burned and muscles contracted, threatening to crush his bones to dust.

The behemoth's heart shriveled, and then Rhoren fell face-first into the snow.

1. THE FINAL WORD

Rhoren massaged his knuckles as the carriage bumped along the dirt road. It had been three months since he'd last used his abilities, but his body still ached. The current pain was nowhere near as bad as when he called upon his magic, but for the past few years, the pain never seemed to fully subside.

He wondered if it ever would.

The carriage came to a halt, and he grabbed his bags. He checked the interior pocket once again for his father's notebook before stepping onto the snowy streets of Hollowton. The snow-covered rooftops blazed in the midday sun, possibly the last snow of the spring, and a trail of footprints led to the door of Olde Gadric's Inn.

This was the first time he'd returned home in over thirty years. Not since that night of terror. The one that had changed everything for him.

The snow crunched beneath his boots, hiding those memories underneath. The town was unrecognizable and unremarkable, not that he expected much else. Of the six years he spent in this small town on the outskirts of civilization, the memories of his last night here were the ones that remained.

Rhoren pushed open the heavy wooden door to the inn and a bell jingled, announcing his entry. The warm air of the hearth welcomed him, but the tavern downstairs was nearly empty aside from a group of four in the back. They laughed and bantered, paying no mind to the elf as he approached the bar.

The bartender's features were similar to Rhoren's, with the dark skin, black hair, and slightly pointed ears of the umbral elves. His reddish eyes looked up from the glass he was polishing, giving Rhoren a quizzical look. "Not many officers take this route up north." He gestured toward the group in the back. "This is more adventurer territory."

Rhoren looked over his shoulder, taking in the group for a second time. There was a broad-shouldered man with fiery red hair, a stout dwarf, and a slender elven female with the alabaster skin of the elder elves. The fourth member of their party was shorter in stature and had their face hidden beneath a hood.

They could have their adventures. He'd had enough for a lifetime.

Rhoren ran his finger over the emblem embroidered into his cloak that denoted him as an officer on the northern front. He set his bag down and took a seat on the stool, flashing the bartender a smile. "As of three days ago, my days in the Guard are behind me."

"Cheers to that." The bartender poured him a frothy

mug of ale and set it on the counter. "This one's on the house. For your service. Name's Ehris."

"Rhoren."

"It takes a special type to join the Northern Guard. Been some thirty-odd years since our last attack. Well, from one of the big ones, you know. This lot can fend off the bandits and lesser threats, but if you ask me, it's you folks that keep the nine kingdoms from crumbling."

If he only knew…

Rhoren nodded to the umbral elf before lifting the hefty mug. He remembered the last time a behemoth had attacked Hollowton all too well. He squeezed the mug extra hard until his hands burned, putting those thoughts to rest. The warm, malty, and slightly sweet ale put him at ease. He'd heard they drink their ale cold in the south, but up here, they took all the warmth they could get.

Ehris leaned on the counter. "What's next for you? You have a family, or should I introduce you to the fellas in the back? I hear they are gearing up for their next quest. It's almost pruning season in the wilds."

Rhoren took another swig. He wasn't quite sure what was next. After spending most of his life in the Northern Guard, he was free of that responsibility, and this was the only place he'd thought to go. Ten years of training, twenty years of service, and now it was all gone. He'd meet with a cleric in the morning with the hope of finding some guidance, and, if he was lucky, perhaps relief. If he kept his abilities at bay, there was no reason he couldn't live a long life.

He flexed his fingers. "I appreciate the offer, but my fighting days are behind me. Not sure what awaits me next, but I've spilled enough blood for a lifetime."

The bartender nodded gravely. "Not much happens in Hollowton, but you're welcome to a room for as long as you'd like. Three silver per night and that includes dinner." He set the polishing rag on the counter. "Say, you sure you've never passed through here? You look awfully familiar."

"I grew up here." He paused, deciding how much of himself he wanted to reveal. "Before the attack."

"Ah, many good folk died defending the town that night. More went south in the aftermath. The town has been a husk of itself ever since." He scrunched his brow. "They said the damned beast died of a heart attack. Can you believe that? I hate to think how bad it could have been."

Rhoren took another swig of his ale. This wasn't a conversation he wanted to have.

The bartender took notice. "I'll say no more of it, but I hope you gave them hell for what they did to us."

While the elf meandered behind the bar, organizing bottles and glasses, Rhoren pulled out the notebook from his satchel. The binding was a worn, dull leather scarred from years of travel. A leather thong wrapped around a knob on the front, keeping the pages locked within.

Rhoren ran his hands over the front, feeling the aged leather—his last connection to his life before the Guard. The only connection he had to his family.

The notebook had belonged to his father, who, in his youth, had traveled across the realm spending his days taking odd jobs and his nights in various taverns. He'd had a passion for drinks, cocktails in particular, and had filled the pages with notes, sketches, and recipes. Ingredients were limited so far to the north, but Rhoren had often envisioned the days when he could put the recipes to use.

He unwound the thong and opened the notebook. The first page contained an inscription.

One day, when these pages are filled and my travels are done, I hope to open my own tavern and share its contents with the world. -Dhorian Balsalor

Rhoren stared at his father's handwriting. He could no longer remember his voice, but there was still life to his words. On those cold nights in the far north, Rhoren remembered the elf who had faced down a behemoth to protect his son. This notebook had given Rhoren the strength to go on when his body burned and the pain of blood magic threatened to consume him.

His father's words had kept him going. He pressed his finger to the long-dried ink and could almost remember his face.

Almost.

Rhoren turned the page, revealing the first recipe his father had written in the book.

The Final Word

Ingredients:

1 oz Lime Juice
1 oz Cherry Liqueur
1 oz Tiberian Monk's Herbal Elixir (green)
1 oz Dry Jin

Underneath, his father had scribbled tasting notes and other information about the drink.

Taste: *Refreshing, tart, and with a subtle sweetness. The herbal liqueur from the Tiberian Monks brings a hint of bitterness that meshes with the ripe fruit of the cherry liqueur.*

Appearance: *Yellowish-green. Ungarnished or served with a lime peel on the rim.*

Created by Wilbur Barcall, tavern owner of The Industrious Pig in Tiberia. When a traveling monk traded a stopper of medicinal elixir in exchange for a night at the inn, Wilbur had the inventive idea to test the elixir in one of his concoctions and The Final Word was born. Although the monk's elixirs are extremely hard to procure under normal circumstances, Wilbur made an agreement with the monks to receive a bottle of their elixir every fortnight in exchange for keeping a single room reserved for traveling monks.

The notes went on and on, dozens upon dozens of drink recipes detailing their taste, appearance, history, and so much more. Rhoren had combed over them hundreds of times. His father had been a studious man, much more than Rhoren had ever dared. He wondered if he would ever be as passionate about anything as his father was about drinks.

Rhoren waved the bartender over, turning around the notebook and pointing at the recipe. "Any chance you could make one of these?"

Thirty years he'd had the notebook, and he'd yet to

taste a single drink from within. Ale was plentiful on the northern front, but it was always the same—strong and sweet.

Ehris leaned closer, furrowing his brow as he read through the ingredients. He shook his head. "I've got the jin, that's about it. Limes and cherry liqueur don't travel this far north, and I've never heard of the other one. You may have better luck in a bigger city."

Rhoren took the notebook back. "Thanks, it was worth a shot."

Ehris smiled. "Whoever wrote that sure had a passion for drinks."

"It belonged to my father."

"Hmm." Ehris scratched his chin. "If you let me take a look, there might be something in there I can whip up. I've got limited ingredients, but you never know."

Rhoren drank his ale while Ehris perused the contents, occasionally tapping his chin or making a note on a piece of parchment. When he was done, he slid the notebook back across the bar.

"Your father lived a fruitful life, that's for sure. It's not often an umbral elf travels the realm like he did." He smiled again. "I don't have all the ingredients, but I'll do my take on one of your father's recipes. Listen for the dinner bell at dusk."

Rhoren pulled three silver and one gold coin from his pocket and placed it on the bar before gathering his things. "I'll take a room for the night."

Ehris's eyes widened as he stared at the additional piece of gold that would cover nearly a week's worth of room and board. A struggle played out behind the elf's eyes, but in the end, he only took the three silver. "There's no need for that."

Rhoren slid the gold coin forward. "For your kindness."

And then he went to his room for the evening.

2. MULLED WINE

The gong of the dinner bell roused Rhoren from an evening nap. As he made his way down to the tavern, the smell of fresh bread drifted up the stairs. His stomach rumbled.

Nearly a dozen people were now scattered about the lower level. Candles flickered among the tables and walls, and a bard plucked on a lute between sips of ale. Dark hair draped across the red eyes of the young umbral elf as he sang about a lady trapped in a lake. A barmaid bustled about, refilling drinks and chatting idly. Even this far north, people still sought community.

The adventuring party hadn't left, and the red-haired human ladled stew from a large kettle simmering in the hearth. Rhoren's mouth watered as chunky pieces of purple carrot and golden potato tumbled into the bowl. At one of the larger tables, the dwarf tore a loaf of bread in half and shared it with the elf. The cloaked member of their party was nowhere to be found. Perhaps they'd followed in Rhoren's footsteps and ventured upstairs for a short rest.

Ehris waved Rhoren over, then stirred a large pot filled with a deep purple liquid. Circles of sliced orange bobbled inside, and steam wafted across the bar, carrying the faint smell of cinnamon, cloves, and nutmeg.

"It's not your father's, but it isn't half bad for this far north." He dipped a mug into the pot, wiped the edge with a rag, and handed it to Rhoren. "Mulled Wine. Won't have lemons until summer, and I had to use dried oranges, but the baker came through with the spices. Go on, let's hear it."

Rhoren's palms warmed around the mug, and the drink gave off a calming, festive aroma. A stick of cinnamon buoyed within the wine while cloves and other spices settled on top. He'd had mulled wine on the front every winter to celebrate the solstice, but it was nothing like this. The warm liquid ignited his mouth with spice and the slightest hint of fruit. Rhoren closed his eyes as the wine trailed down his throat. The sensation was unlike anything he'd ever tasted. It was a calming warmth, like sitting around a fire. The citrus was barely noticeable, but it was there.

Was this what his father enjoyed about his drinks? The nuance and subtlety of a well-crafted concoction. Drunkenness was a state of being, but this... This was an experience.

He imagined his father sitting in a tavern like this one, surrounded by friends as they drank and shared stories. It reminded Rhoren of the friends he'd made up north. Of the friends he'd lost and those who'd left the Guard for better days.

"So?" Ehris looked at him expectantly.

"It's brilliant." Rhoren smiled.

Ehris tapped his fist to the bar, pride radiating from his dull red eyes. "It's not often I'm given reason to test my skills."

"You should do it more often." Rhoren locked eyes with the elf as he took another sip. "It suits you."

The bartender's cheeks reddened. "You should probably have some stew before it's gone. Urgrack might be short, but dwarves have the appetites of direbears."

Rhoren closed his eyes, inhaling the smell of cinnamon yet again. "Ehris."

"Yes?" The bartender raised an eyebrow.

"This is too delicious to keep to myself. And too much. Would you mind if I shared with the others?"

Ehris grinned. "It's going to be one of those nights, eh?" He pounded the butt of a thick mug on the counter. The bard quit playing and the chatter died down as everyone turned their attention to the bar. "Tonight is a special occasion. My good friend Rhoren has just earned his retirement from the Northern Guard. I've made a celebratory drink on his behalf, and he's a better elf than I, because he's offered to share it with the likes of you."

"Hear, hear!" The red-haired adventurer beat his fist on the table, followed by cheers from around the tavern.

The dwarf stuffed the remaining bread in his mouth and leapt across the table, talking with a full mouth. "Yeh don't have to tell me twice." He shoved his way through the crowd, earning dirty looks and patting Rhoren on the backside as he passed. "Have a seat with us and tell us all about your adventures in the north."

Maybe this hadn't been the best idea after all. Nevertheless, he joined the adventurers at their table, where several other patrons came by to toast him and offer their thanks. The elder elf scooped Rhoren a bowl of stew and sat across from him as the dwarf rejoined the table with three mugs of mulled wine, handing them to his party.

He lifted his mug. "To Rhoren, and whatever comes next."

"I like that." Rhoren tapped his mug to each of theirs in turn. "To whatever comes next." Then, he shifted the focus away before they could barrage him with personal questions. "So, Ehris tells me you lot are adventurers."

One thing all adventurers had in common was how much they loved to talk about themselves.

"Aye." The red-haired human let his spoon fall into his bowl and leaned forward, elbows resting on the table. "Pruning season is nearly upon us, and there's coin to be made along the wilds. You can call me Fallahan." He gestured to the dwarf, and then to the elf. "This is Urgrack. And this is the lovely Allayah." He looked around the tavern. "There's no telling where Zef has gotten off to, but together, we're known as Fate's Fortune. We seek gold and glory across the nine kingdoms."

Rhoren was well aware of pruning season, the yearly tradition of clearing back the underbrush along the wilds in order to keep the eastern forest from encroaching upon the rest of Aedrea. The trees within the wilds were so tall and dense that they were said to blot out the sky. The monsters within rivaled the behemoths to the north, but they were more susceptible to flesh wounds. Nothing a well-paid band of adventurers couldn't handle.

He'd never been able to visit the wilds. Blood mages were the only gifted ones capable of going head-to-head with a behemoth, and their place was up north. Behemoth scales were naturally resistant to magical attacks, but blood magic didn't work like most arcane.

Rhoren ate his fill of stew as Fallahan and Urgrack took turns detailing their exploits, from hunting monsters in Stormrest to seeking treasure among the haunted ruins of Hells' Crag. The group had certainly traveled the realm.

Hours passed, but eventually, they got back around to Rhoren.

Surprisingly, it was Allayah who asked the question, her blue eyes staring intently into his own. "What's next for a warrior as seasoned as yourself? To survive twenty years in the frozen north is no easy feat."

Again, he had no waiting answer. "I suppose that is what I intend to find out. The north is all I've ever known."

She flashed him a mischievous smile. "The life of an adventurer isn't so different from a soldier. You get all of the action, but there's no one giving you orders. Plus, the pay's better."

"Coin is the least of my concern." Underneath the table, he flexed his aching hand. Blood mages were compensated well, an unfair bargain for losing their lives to the cause. Most didn't live long enough to spend a copper, much less twenty years' worth. He had enough money to live a simple life for the rest of his days, or to go out in an extravagant blaze over the course of a few years. What he lacked was purpose.

"Glory, then?" Fallahan placed an arm on Rhoren's shoulder. "The Blood Guardians are the only ones who have songs written about them up north. They say the Bloodbane is an umbral elf."

Rhoren nearly choked on his mulled wine. Blood Guardians, the Cursed Ones, Walking Death. There were a dozen names for his kind. The soldiers had told him of the songs sung in the northern taverns while on their leave. The songs of Bloodbane, the umbral elf blood mage and his feats against the behemoths. At the time, he hadn't believed it.

"You alright there?" Fallahan patted Rhoren on the back as he hacked and coughed.

Rhoren cleared his throat. "Yes, sorry. Must have been the clove. There's a song about the Bloodbane?"

"Songs about him and many of the blood mages." The red-haired adventurer nodded. "You know him?"

"I know of him," Rhoren lied.

"Oi!" Urgrack shouted for the bard. "Play the ballad of Bloodbane."

"Am I taking requests now?" The bard frowned at the dwarf, jingling a cup filled with a single coin.

"It's for Rhoren. The one who shared his mulled wine with your sorry arse."

The bard grinned. "For wine like this, I'll play anything you want."

He strummed the lute and the notes carried across the tavern, drowning out the chatter. The elf's voice was beautiful, and Rhoren lost himself in the words of the song.

"In the north beyond the trees,
  among frigid cold, snow and ice,
  the Northern Guard is all that stands
  between true terror and our lands.

· · ·

Brave and bold, they hold the line,
so that the realm may sleep at night.
Monsters lurk, behemoths prey,
but the Guard holds them at bay.

There is one who leads the charge.
Powered by magic most mortals fear.
He is the bane of monstrous evil.
He is the guardian of our people.

Bloodbane, defender of the realm.
Blood Guardian, sends them down to hell.
His veins are cursed, his body torn.
But still, he fights for you and yourn.

With anguished cries, behemoths fall.
And other terrors fear the call.
For none escape the Bloodbane's reaper.
He guards the north, our sacred keeper."

The song continued for several more refrains, and when it ended, Rhoren found a heavy weight had settled on his shoulders. Although tonight had been wonderful with delicious drinks, a nice meal, and a warm tavern with new friends, he wondered if he should have stayed on the front, if he should have given his life to the realm since there were precious few who could.

"You know, we've had a few songs written about us."

Urgrack pulled Rhoren from his thoughts.

Rhoren raised a brow. "You don't say?"

The dwarf turned to the bard. "What do you say you play the song of Fate's Fortune."

The bard rolled his eyes. "How many times do I have to tell you? You can't request your own song."

3. BLOODBANE

Like so much of the town, the temple was empty aside from the dwarven cleric who knelt before the altar. Several statues looked down from the pulpit, and stained-glassed windows brought color to the otherwise dreary gray walls. Rhoren's footsteps echoed throughout the building, and the cleric stirred.

A short, stout dwarf with a braided black beard smiled at Rhoren. He pressed the creases from his robe as he stood. "Bloodbane."

Rhoren stopped halfway down the aisle, wondering what the dwarf was doing in Hollowton. "Those days are behind me."

The cleric's smile widened. "You're one of the few Blood Guardians who've survived long enough to earn your retirement. Your name will live longer than you do. They sang of you last night as I walked past the inn."

"What are you doing here, Charence?" Rhoren cut right to the chase. The cleric had spent more time on the northern front than any other. If he was out here, then something was up.

"Now, now. That's no way to treat an old friend." He sighed. "Look, I was in Durendreg dealing with a nasty bit of, well, let's just say the dead were refusing to stay that way. When I learned of your retirement, I wanted to pay my respects to you one final time."

"Respects, huh?" Rhoren sat on one of the pews. "Is my situation that dire?"

Charence walked over and joined him. "Quite the contrary. I'd say your situation has never been better. Avoiding the constant threat of death and dismemberment will do wonders for one's lifespan."

Rhoren raised an eyebrow. "Come to tell me how lucky I am then?"

"Luck. Almost as whimsical as the gods." The cleric patted him on the leg. "No, I wanted to wish you well. For all you've given to the realm, I'd chop off my own hand if it could cure you of your pain. I've seen many of your kind go mad with the price. I've seen more…" He sighed. "Well, you know. Precious few embrace their abilities in the way you have. If it were up to any one of the nine kingdoms, you'd still be at the front, fighting until you no longer could. But the Guard recognizes your sacrifices."

Rhoren glanced at him sideways. "You always did love to ramble on."

"And you always loved to brood, but fine, I'll get on with it." Charence shook his head. "You know by now not even I can cure you. I brought potions and elixirs that can help manage your pain, but they don't work forever. Your powers, the same ones that have protected the realm from untold atrocities, have cursed your very being. Every time you invoke them, the damage will only worsen."

"Aren't you a ray of sunshine." Rhoren frowned. "I hope you didn't come all this way to tell me what I already know."

"I came to tell you that there may be another way." Charence let the words hang in the air.

Rhoren's throat caught. There was a reason blood mages were referred to as the Cursed Ones. Not even a cleric could reverse the damage that blood magic wreaked upon his body. Pain had become his default over the years. It pulsed uneasily in his joints even now. He knew the dangers of relying too heavily on elixirs and potions and avoided them as much as possible. "What do you mean?"

"There's reason to believe that northern climates react harshly with certain conditions. I never wanted to give you false hope during your service, but now that it's over, I feel I can be frank with you. There are others, not blood mages, but they have found relief from incurable curses in warmer climates. We don't know why, but something about these locations sets their bodies at ease. There's nothing for you to lose by trying."

Rhoren leaned against the wooden pew. A pain-free life. It sounded too good to be true, which probably meant it was. But still, Charence had come all this way to speak to him, and he was a dwarf of the gods, after all. He'd seen Rhoren through the highs and lows of the northern front.

"South, huh? Do you really think it could put me at ease?"

"I don't know." His gaze lingered on the statue of

Melora, Goddess of the Harvest. "But I doubt it would cause you more pain."

Rhoren's eyes followed the cleric's, where the goddess cradled a cornucopia of fruit and vegetables in her arms. Of all the places for her to be, Hollowton seemed like the last one she'd ever grace with her presence. "What do the gods say?"

Charence sighed. "The gods say little as of late. Some in my order believe we are entering a new Age of Enlightenment, and the gods have set us down our own path."

Rhoren fought the urge to roll his eyes. "And what do you believe?"

The cleric looked at him from the corner of his eye. "I believe that after seventy-eight years in their service, I still know precious little regarding the wills of the gods."

Rhoren smiled, revisiting the cleric's proposition once again. "Are you certain I won't turn to mush in the heat?"

"Find a nice beach, let your hair blow in the wind." Charence winked. "There are worse places to retire."

"Retirement." Rhoren shook his head. "I never thought the day would come, and now that it has, I'm not sure I earned it. It feels like there is still work to be done."

Charence placed a hand on Rhoren's shoulder. "The work is never done, that's the part that gets you. But if anyone has earned a retirement, it's you. There's no telling how many lives you have saved."

Rhoren sat in silence for a long moment, contemplating. Even if a warmer climate couldn't cure his ills, there was little to lose by trying. He'd finally have a chance to see the world of Aedrea, and if Ehris was right, a bigger city might allow him to try a few more of his father's cocktails. That in itself would be worth the trip.

"Alright, Charence, tell me more about these southern climates."

4. NELDERLAND MULE

The trip to the Tiberian Peninsula was long and boring, and after two months of travel by carriage, Rhoren began to curse Charence with every bump in the road. The coachman was nice enough, but the dwarf seemed to enjoy his own company more than Rhoren's. He would sing for hours on end, epic songs of ale and women, or talk to his pet raven, which cawed incessantly in reply. The snow of the north soon turned to rain and mud, and Rhoren began to wonder if this was all part of some elaborate trick to lure him back to the Guard.

But when he was greeted by the smell of saltwater, his ill will evaporated into the ether. A sprawling stretch of deep blue sea vanished against the horizon unlike anything he'd ever seen. Two more weeks passed before he arrived on the cobbled streets of Eastborne with excitement and fervor for his new life.

The city was far bigger than any town he'd ever visited. Etched into the coastline of the rugged countryside, the city seemed to rise from the sea itself. A massive harbor ran along the bay, and ships dotted the horizon.

They entered the city, where multi-story buildings towered above the tiered streets. A river ran through the center, and as they continued the ascent, almost every section offered a picturesque view of the bay. They passed a market so full of fresh produce and vendors that Rhoren's pockets felt lighter just by looking, and the streets were full of people who seemed to not have a care in the world.

The carriage came to a stop outside of the Seaside Inn, which sat above the mountainous coastline overlooking the sea. Rhoren stretched his arms overhead, admiring the water as it sparkled in the fading sun. Tomorrow, he would begin to look for long-term accommodations, but for tonight, he was in search of a hearty meal and a good drink.

The Seaside Inn and Tavern was luxurious in ways Rhoren had never imagined. With thick polished wood and immaculately kept quarters, it was opulence he'd never experienced on the northern front. Charence had recommended this place, and it made Rhoren wonder what company the cleric kept when he wasn't with the Guard.

After a hot bath to wash away the stench of travel, he joined the bustling tavern downstairs. Although East-borne was in the human kingdom of Nelderland, the patrons were from far and wide. In addition to the many humans, a group of rowdy dwarves wearing fine linens tossed back ale by the pitcher. A couple of gnomes drank wine while analyzing a piece of parchment, and a lone halfling sat in an oversized chair blowing smoke rings from a pipe.

There was no roaring fire, but elaborate sconces flickered around the tavern. Beautiful tapestries hung along the walls, and in one corner, a minstrel played soothing music that set the whole place at ease.

After years in the hard north, Rhoren felt out of place, so he took a seat at the bar. Perhaps a drink would calm his nerves. The raven-haired bartender who had greeted him on arrival was gone, replaced by a man with a thick but well-maintained beard. His youthful face contradicted the silver of his facial hair.

The man winked a piercing blue eye at Rhoren as he sat. "What'll it be, handsome?"

The bartender slid a piece of parchment across the counter that listed ale, wine, and cocktails Rhoren had never heard of. He was thinking about asking for whatever the dwarves were drinking when the man spoke again.

"We don't get many of you around here."

Rhoren narrowed his eyes. Charence had assured him that the umbral elves were no longer treated with disdain throughout the realm.

"Soldiers." The man threw up his hands. "I'm sorry, that came out wrong. We don't get many soldiers around here. You're a long way from the frozen north." He pointed to the emblem on Rhoren's tunic.

The tension released from Rhoren's shoulders. Everything he owned had the insignia of the Northern Guard on it. "No need to apologize. I've been traveling for ages."

The man smiled. "I don't envy that ride. Traveling from Eastborne to Tiberia is enough for me to never want to leave the city again. Name's Kallum. What brings you all the way to Eastborne?"

Rhoren shook the man's hand. "Rhoren. I guess you could say this is my chance at a new beginning."

"Cheers to that, Rhoren. You've certainly come to the right place. Eastborne is a city of transplants and dreamers." He tossed a bar rag over his shoulder. "So, what'll it be?"

Rhoren pushed the parchment a few inches away. As much as he'd read through his father's notebook, it did little to help him understand what the ingredients actually tasted like or what he wanted. "What do you recommend? My knowledge of spirits is lacking, to say the least."

The bartender leaned forward, turning the parchment in his direction. "Well, luckily for you, I handpicked every item on this list myself."

Rhoren glanced at the parchment. "Is that so?"

"Truly. Timofey might own the inn, but I run the tavern. Our chef handles the food menu, and I take care of the drinks. So, what do you like?"

Rhoren laughed. "I'm not even sure I know. We mostly drank ale up north. Mulled wine on special occasions."

"No need to worry. I'll be your tour guide through the land of spirits this evening."

A slender elder elf approached the bar, and Kallum motioned for one of the barmaids to top off her glass of ruby red wine.

Kallum returned his attention to Rhoren. "This top section has your various ales. Dark stouts from the mountain dwarves of Rockdale and porters from Drake Canyon. With flavors of chocolate, coffee, and peanut butter, they're like a meal in a glass. If you prefer something lighter, Stormrest and Wolfwater both brew some of the crispest lagers in the nine realms. The gnomes love their ciders, but I find them too sweet for my taste. I get the sense that if you're staying in a place like this, ale is not what you're in the mood for after such a long journey."

Rhoren flashed him a wry smile. "I see why Timofey chose you."

"Don't flatter me just yet. There is still much to narrow down." He traced his finger down the parchment to a section full of wines.

Rhoren sat up straight. "By all means, don't let me hinder you."

"Wine." Kallum let the word hang in the air. "There may be a beer for every occasion, but there is a wine for every mood. Sparkling wines of Crowhold. The icewine of Aethervale. Even the halflings have their version of white wine that tastes of honey and floral notes. The elder elves have perfected the dry reds. Even your people have their own varietals. Wine is as old as the kingdoms themselves. While I find your true drink for the evening, I will sample you with a sparkling wine from Bearmouth. You wouldn't think it, but the lowland dwarves have an affinity for celebratory toasts."

Kallum slid back a lid from a large metal box situated behind the bar and frigid air rose from within. He pulled out a frosty bottle with the upper half wrapped in foil. As he wiped his finger across the label, ice crystals flaked around his finger.

With a flourish, he presented the bottle to Rhoren in outstretched hands. The label had an illustration of a roaring bear head encircled with pink flowers and vines.

"A sparkling rosado from Bearmouth chilled to perfection." Kallum placed a flute glass on the bar and peeled the foil from the top of the bottle, revealing a cork wrapped with wire. "There's a lot of pressure within these, so best to point it away if you value your eyesight."

With a finger pressed to the top of the cork, he untwisted the wire and carefully removed it. Without breaking eye contact, he gently twisted the cork until a hiss escaped. "Most people open them violently to where the contents explode like a geyser. If the celebration calls for such extravagance, fine, but you're wasting a damn good wine."

He tilted the bottle until a light pink liquid poured into the flute. Bubbles filled the top half of the glass, but the wine underneath fogged the flute with its chill.

"How do you keep it so cold in these climates?" asked Rhoren.

"The gnomes grow more industrious by the day. Their newest invention is called a chiller. I hate to guess how much it set Timofey back, but it's worth every gold." He nodded to Rhoren. "To new beginnings."

Rhoren lifted the wine and small bubbles misted his nose as he took a sip. Fresh notes of strawberry and crisp apple settled while floral notes of winter rose washed over him before the effervescence faded with a refreshing, clean finish.

"Wow."

"Not bad, eh? We're just getting started."

Rhoren took another sip. "This would have been worth the stay in itself. I can't imagine you can top this."

"Oh, my new friend, then you are in for a world of surprise." He pushed the parchment back in front of

Rhoren and grabbed several bottles from the back shelf, placing them on the counter before him. "Anyone can pour a shot, but to really understand the ingredients, to create a cocktail, now that is art. No different than a potion or elixir brewed by a competent mage."

There was a passion in Kallum's eyes that reminded Rhoren of his father. The way he talked so reverently about cocktails was the same respect that he read on every page of his father's journal.

Kallum continued. "Every cocktail starts with its base, whether that be jin, watka, wuiskey, rhum, or mezcalium, or one of the lesser-known spirits. Each one brings a unique flavor to the drink. I could bore you with the histories and regional differences of each one, but I will leave it at this. You can learn a lot about a person's personality from the alcohol they consume, and when I design a drink, I want the person drinking it to feel like their truest self."

Rhoren finished off the last of his rosado and placed the flute gently to the bar. "Well, then, give me your best."

Kallum smiled devilishly. "Very well then." He tapped the tops of the five liquor bottles in turn. "A member of the Northern Guard who has traveled as far south as he could in search of a new beginning. I'd wager you aren't only searching for a fresh start but a direction. After countless years of taking orders, you're unsure of how to live a life of complete freedom."

Rhoren watched as Kallum finally settled on a bottle. Though he might have come south to ease his suffering, there was some truth to the man's words. He was a leaf in the wind, far from the branches he once called home.

Kallum continued. "At its core, watka is the most

simple liquor. Originally fermented from potatoes by the halflings, it can now be found in taverns all across the realm. I've always found watka to be the most boundless of all spirits. It can be consumed as a straight shot after a hard day's work, mixed with tomato juice and spices to start one's day of relaxation, or mixed with a coffee liqueur as a tasty nightcap. Watka can make the best of any situation. To survive the north, I imagine you can as well. So for you, I recommend the Nelderland Mule. When you find your direction, you'll need a way to get there."

Kallum removed a copper mug from a rack and set it on the bar, the polished metal reflecting the candles around the room. "The Nelderland Mule is one of the traditional cocktails of our kingdom and is always served in a copper mug. The copper takes the cold better than glass, and it adds an additional element to the drink."

He reached into the chiller and pulled out a block of ice the size of his head, setting it on a cutting board. With a chisel, he flaked off pieces of ice and then placed them in the mug, where frost gathered on the outside.

Rhoren narrowed his eyes as Kallum poured a generous amount of watka, followed by an even more generous amount of an amber liquid that fizzed within the cup.

"Ginger beer. Spicy and refreshing." He grinned as he squeezed juice from a fresh lime, and placed a lime wheel on the edge of the mug. "I get the feeling you are a simple elf at heart, but even so, there are complexities to you that the world doesn't see." He gave the drink a quick stir and flourish before placing it in front for Rhoren.

Rhoren took the handle in one hand and pressed the

other to the cool exterior for a moment, leaving the imprint of his hand. The first sip was refreshingly citrus, followed by the lingering spiciness of ginger beer. When the taste faded, he found himself smiling.

"That might be the best drink I've ever had."

"I aim to please." Kallum swept his arm as he bowed. "I'll let you enjoy your drink. Let me know if you would like to order any food."

Rhoren sat at the bar enjoying his cocktail and taking in the other patrons as the night wore on. He had another Nelderland Mule, followed by a delicious dinner of roasted fish and vegetables. He wasn't sure if it was the freshness of the ingredients or the quality of the cooking, but everything seemed to taste better here.

He looked forward to seeing what else the city had to offer. Starting with more permanent accommodations.

5. THE COPPER WHEEL

Rhoren awoke feeling better than he had in quite some time. The bed in his room at the Seaside Inn was softer than anything he'd ever slept upon. He could certainly get used to a life away from the Guard. Bones cracked as he stretched his arms overhead. His knuckles still burned, but the flare of pain in his shoulder joints felt duller than usual.

"Maybe Charence was right," Rhoren said as he combed his hair in the mirror.

He'd had a wonderful evening relaxing and chatting with the bartender the night before, but today, he wanted to see the city. First, he needed more appropriate attire for the climate, and then he'd explore the city for permanent accommodations.

After a delicious breakfast of fresh fruit and seasoned potatoes, Rhoren set off in search of a tailor. There were numerous options in a city of this size, but he settled on one in the same district as the Seaside Inn. Traveling on foot made him aware of just how thick his clothing really was. Perspiration clung to his charcoal skin as he entered the Plum Crazy Boutique.

The shop was filled with clothing in more styles, shapes, and colors than Rhoren could have imagined. On the northern front, everyone wore black or brown, aside from the clerics. Even in Hollowton, people never ventured far beyond shades of gray or green. And ruffles, he laughed as he felt the soft fabric, ruffles were unheard of. Wool, fur, and leather were how northerners survived.

There were leggings and gowns—for both women and men, apparently. Hats with flamboyant feathers, and others, called chaperones, that looked like a piece of cloth had been draped over the mannequin's head.

Rhoren kept to his usual style, replacing his pants, tunic, and cloaks of the Northern Guard with lighter and slightly more colorful versions. He left the store in a pair of tan pants and a blue tunic.

With his old clothing stuffed in a cotton bag with a plum painted on the outside, Rhoren flagged down a rickshaw. The raven-haired young man pulling the cart had broad shoulders and even thicker thighs. No doubt from carrying passengers up and down the tiered streets of Eastborne.

The young man wiped his brow as he let the passenger cart come to a stop. "Good day, sir. Where is it you're headed?"

Rhoren looked out over the tiered city, unsure. "To be honest, I don't really know. I'm new to the city, and I was hoping to get the lay of the land." He pulled a gold coin from his pouch. "I'd make it worth your while if you'd give me the tour."

The young man nodded. "Might be I could make that happen. Hop on in."

Rhoren climbed into the passenger cart, and the young man took one of the handles in each hand, slowly pulling it along, talking as he walked. "Eastborne is a good city. Plenty of opportunity if you know where to look. Pulling a cart might not seem like much, but it's honest work, and it sure beats farming. What is it you do, mister? Might help me take you to the right places."

Rhoren took in the city as the cart bumped along, a nice breeze passing through the cotton fabric of his new clothes. From their current location, he could see most of Eastborne, all the way down to the docks and far out to sea. "For now, I'm just seeing the sights. Not sure what I'll be doing after that."

"Been here before?"

"First time."

"Aye, well, first thing you should know is that the river runs right through the middle, not that you couldn't see for yourself. Some say we got two cities in Eastborne, but I don't see it that way. I may live across the river, but the folks over here treat me alright. This here is the Noble District. It has the best inns and taverns in the city, the best shops, and most of the more wealthy folks call it home. Behind us is the Council District with the city keep. That's the only place you might have a hard time getting into. That's where Lord Heyden and the councilmembers live."

As they traveled around the city, the young man—Jesper—proved to be a wealth of knowledge regarding Eastborne's layout. On the northern side of the river were the Trade, Art, and University Districts, the Premier

Market, civic buildings, temples, and various guild halls. The library in the University District was one of the tallest buildings in the city, and the Art District had musicians and street performers all throughout the day. Most of the middle and upper class lived north of the river.

Three bridges connected the two sides, and Jesper stopped before one of them to point out the southern half of the city on the other side. There were the stables and tannery, the two smelliest locations, along with the Warehouse District, and a separate walled district for the alchemists, who had been moved across the river the last time an unforeseen explosion had leveled a city block.

"If you dabble with the unsavory sort, the Warehouse District is where you'll find them," Jesper added.

At the river's mouth were the docks, and the second largest port in Nelderland. A handful of ships could be seen speckling the sea, coming and going.

Jesper took a swig from his water flask and readied the cart.

Rhoren held up a hand. "We've been at this for a while. What do you say we grab lunch? It's on me."

Jesper grinned. "I've never turned down a meal. Where to?"

"How about you pick? I'm sure you'll do a much better job than me."

A few minutes later, Jesper parked his cart outside of a restaurant with a large sign in the shape of a wheel over the door. "It's called the Copper Wheel. They have the best flatbread in the city."

Whatever they were cooking inside, it smelled absolutely divine. Rhoren's mouth watered as Jesper combed through his sweaty hair with his fingers and pressed his clothing with callused hands before gesturing for Rhoren to lead the way.

Flatbread, it turned out, was exactly as it sounded. A circle of flat dough topped with a layer of tomato sauce, an assortment of toppings, and finished with cheese. The dough was then put in an oven until the flatbread formed a crispy crust and the cheese melted. Then it was cut into several slices and eaten by hand.

The Copper Wheel was busy, but not crowded, and it seemed that each table had their own take on the flatbread's toppings. Rhoren and Jesper sat at a table underneath an open-air patio with a view of the city and the sea. A pitcher of cool lager from Wolfwater sat on the table next to a flatbread topped with various meats and vegetables. Jesper called it the Supreme.

It smelled so good that Rhoren took a bite without waiting, the hot cheese burning the roof of his mouth. He gaped like a fish in an attempt to cool it down, but the taste soon made him forget about the momentary pain.

"Gods," he said between bites. "This is amazing."

Jesper stuffed a slice in his mouth, devouring half of it with one bite. "Oh, it's wonderful, an Eastborne specialty. There are so many ways to order it, too."

"I can't imagine it being any better than this." He cooled his burnt mouth with a swig of refreshing ale. "I appreciate you giving me the tour of the city today. How long have you called Eastborne home?"

Jesper wiped foam from his upper lip. "Going on three years now."

"You mentioned farming earlier. Is that what you did before?"

"It is. Once my father passed, it was time for me to

move on. I never really felt like I belonged on a farm, so I sold it along with all of the livestock and was able to buy my own place down by the docks. It was an adjustment at first, but Eastborne has been the best thing to ever happen to me." He gestured to the window overlooking the sea. "This isn't a sight you can see just anywhere, and we get to see it every day."

Rhoren smiled at Jesper's optimism. He'd seen grim faces far too often up north. "I'm looking to call Eastborne home for a while myself. Do you know of anywhere with a room for rent in the upper districts?"

He wasn't opposed to living in the outer districts, or even across the river if it came to it, but even in his short time here, he was getting accustomed to the finer things in life.

Jesper shook his head. "Can't say I do. Those that move here don't often leave, but I'll keep my ear to the ground for you." He suddenly frowned. "Unless..." The words trailed off.

Rhoren leaned forward. "Unless what?"

Jesper gave him a sheepish look. "There might be one place. It's right in the center of the Trade District."

"That sounds perfect." Rhoren grinned. The Trade District surrounded the Premier Market to the north and was at the epicenter of all the best places in Eastborne. "So, what's the problem?"

Jesper leaned forward, whispering, "People say it's cursed."

Rhoren was unable to hold in his laugh. "What makes you say that?"

"I'm serious." Jesper's face indicated he believed it. "The apartment is connected to a storefront on the ground floor. There have been five shops there just since I've been in the city. Nothing ever lasts more than a few months. The last one, a cute lady with a spice shop, hired me to drive her down to the port once she gave up. She said there were always noises at night. She'd come downstairs and find spices knocked to the floor or things rearranged. Could be wraiths, or specters, or maybe even shadow fairies. Whatever it is, the building has been empty for three months now. I guess no one wants to try their luck."

Rhoren grinned. It would take more than a few spilled spices to scare him off. "Show me."

6. SUGAR, SPICE, AND EVERYTHING NICE

The sign for Sugar, Spice, and Everything Nice still hung above the door of the abandoned storefront, though the shop's contents had been long emptied. There were shelves and tables inside, a few pieces of parchment strewn about, and a handful of empty jars, but nothing else as far as Rhoren could see by peeking through the window.

Upstairs, a small balcony and large windows overlooked the Trade District. Rhoren could already imagine himself sitting there in the morning, drinking tea as he prepared to start his day of leisure.

Jesper stood down by his cart, not venturing anywhere near the storefront. A few passersby gave Rhoren a curious look, some even shaking their heads as they walked away.

Rhoren had fought monsters that would keep them up at night, and there was little chance that anything within this building could frighten him. Real terrors didn't hide inside of spice shops.

"Do you happen to know who owns this property?" Rhoren asked as he rejoined Jesper.

Jesper's eyes widened. "You're actually considering it?"

"With this view—" He gestured toward the market and the rest of the city. "—I don't care if it is cursed."

"Then you're crazier than you look."

After years of venturing into the snowy depths of the north, that was probably true.

While Jesper didn't know who owned the property, Rhoren didn't think it would take much digging to find out. He'd start by asking Kallum when he returned to the Seaside Inn. If that proved fruitless, he could venture to city hall.

Twilight was upon the city by the time they arrived back at the inn.

"If you see me around, don't be a stranger," Rhoren said as he paid Jesper for the day's work of chauffeuring him around.

He was watching Jesper pull his cart down the street when a loud clatter in the alley caught his attention. Rhoren peeked around the corner, and saw a man across the alley pacing next to some overturned crates. It was a moment before he recognized the silver of Kallum's beard.

"Everything okay?" he asked.

Kallum clenched his fist, taking a deep breath. "Yeah, I'm good." He took another breath, opened his mouth, reconsidered, and then finally spoke. "I've put years of my life into this place, and I don't ask for much. You'd think building up one of the best drink menus in all of Eastborne would earn me a little respect. I just—" He seemed suddenly aware that he was venting. "I'm sorry. You're supposed to spill your troubles to me, not the other way around."

"It's fine." Rhoren squeezed Kallum on the shoulder. "Why don't you make me a drink and you can tell me all about it?"

Kallum laughed. "Remember, you asked for it."

Inside, a barmaid scurried around the inn, lighting the sconces for the evening. As Rhoren walked to the bar, he passed a purple-haired gnome sitting next to a dark-skinned man. The gnome pointed at a piece of parchment with a stubby finger as she mentioned something about investment opportunities.

This truly was a different world.

Kallum whispered in the ear of the raven-haired bartender. She nodded, pointing to a notepad on the bar before grabbing her things and leaving.

"So, what'll it be today?" Kallum leaned against the bar with a grin.

"I'm in an adventurous mood." Rhoren winked. "Surprise me."

"Adventurous, eh?" Kallum raised an eyebrow. "Did someone enjoy their first day in the city?"

He grabbed a bottle from the shelf, pouring crimson wine into a glass. The turbulent liquid calmed as he slid it across the bar.

Rhoren inhaled the rich, earthy aroma. It reminded him of the forest before the first snow. "I familiarized myself with the layout of the city. Seems I have more refined tastes than I would have thought."

"From soldier to socialite." Kallum grinned. "That's not a transformation you see every day."

Rhoren took a sip. Notes of raspberry, cherry, and the faintest hint of mint coated his tongue.

He tilted the glass to Kallum in acknowledgment. "Once again, delicious."

"A Hillside red. Another specialty of the lowland dwarves." He polished a glass before placing it on the rack. "What did you think of our fair city?"

"I think there is enough to explore to keep me busy for quite some time. And I may have found an apartment, if I can locate the owner."

Kallum tossed a cleaning rag over his shoulder. "Hopefully not too far from here."

"It's in the Trade District." Rhoren chuckled. "Jesper says people believe it's cursed."

"Cursed, eh?" Kallum raised an eyebrow.

Rhoren filled him in on the details, reiterating Jesper's story.

Kallum shrugged. "I know the place. Could be bad business owners, or it could very well be cursed. Either way, I've seen a fair share of shops open and close in that spot over the past few years. You'd be a braver man than me to try your luck, but I do happen to know the owner." He leaned forward, wiping a droplet of water from the bar. "His name is Darvish Goldhammer. He's friends with Timofey, so I've served him over the years. He regrets the day he ever bought that building."

"Goldhammer. Is he dwarven?"

"What gave it away?" Kallum smirked. "The Goldhammer Clan sold iron to Nelderland in the olden days when we were at odds with Warminster. They own a good deal of property in Eastborne and Tiberia as a result. I'll give you his business address before you head out."

"I appreciate it. Now, tell me, what has you kicking crates in the alley before your shift has even started?"

"Just one of those days." Kallum sighed. "I thought it might be time to revamp the menu or at least add a few new items. Timofey thinks if it's not broke, don't fix it. We both got a little heated about it."

Rhoren took another sip of wine, relishing the taste. "He has a point. You've put together a damn fine menu."

"Don't I know it." Kallum scoffed. "I've built it up over years, but what's the point in growing complacent? If I'm not challenging myself, what am I even doing here?"

"You're enriching the lives of everyone who comes into this tavern, for one thing."

"That's kind of you to say." Kallum stared across the tavern. "I know that I'm lucky to work in this establishment. Timofey has given me the opportunity to experiment and grow my craft. Sometimes you just want more, you know? I'd like to take risks without having to ask for permission."

Rhoren wondered if he did understand. Ever since joining the Guard, his life had been scripted. Between training and missions, he always had orders to follow and tasks to complete. The only parts that weren't laid out for him were the actual combat. In those moments, he was the architect of destruction. There was no joy in his work, only the peace of knowing that each behemoth destroyed was one less that could slip through the cracks.

His father, on the other hand, had found a true passion for life. He'd found something he enjoyed and had followed his joy all across Aedrea. He'd tucked it all away when he had a family, but he'd lived a life to be proud of.

Rhoren might be retired, but he was still young—young enough to find his own passion.

"Have you ever thought of opening your own tavern?" he asked.

Kallum's eyes flooded with excitement. "I've dreamed of it ever since I created my first drink, but I could never afford a place like this. This location, these ingredients, the reputation. People come here for the reputation of the Seaside Inn, not because of me."

"I wouldn't be so sure about that." Rhoren winked.

The tavern filled with guests as the night wore on, each one searching for a good drink and a relaxing evening. Rhoren worked his way through more of the drink menu, from fruity cocktails to more spirit-forward ones. He could find no fault with Kallum's creations.

As his head swirled, he watched as the man crafted drinks with refined technique, from the way he mixed the ingredients to the flourish he used when straining the contents into their glasses. Every drink was a performance.

Chatter and laughter filled the tavern, and Rhoren enjoyed every bit of it.

7. GOLDHAMMER ENTERPRISES

The facade of Goldhammer Enterprises was a work of art in itself. Simultaneously elegant and imposing, with the appearance of having been carved from a single slab of stone. Tall, ornately-designed columns ran the height of the three-story structure to where a massive, golden sigil —a double-headed hammer encircled by braided knot-work—gleamed in the morning sun.

Inside, the building was no less magnificent, complete with marble floors, sculptures of famous dwarves, and a mosaic of the Goldhammer Clan sigil upon the floor of the entryway. Towering tapestries and paintings adorned the walls, and a chandelier with over a hundred candles hung from the ceiling. Rhoren half-expected a throne at the back of the room. Instead, a set of stairwells curved around a massive stone desk where a dwarven woman stared at Rhoren with a stern expression.

The Goldhammer Clan did not hide their wealth, and judging by the looks he received as he walked in, Rhoren wasn't their typical clientele. He didn't give off the appearance of a peasant, but he wore no jewelry or elaborate clothing, and his boots were worn from years on the front.

The dwarven woman was short and stout, with flaming red sideburns that framed her chubby face. She wore her hair in two thick braids that wrapped around her head like a crown.

Rhoren approached the desk, passing a pair of humans and an elderly gnome who sat waiting on luxurious leather couches.

"Do you have an appointment?" The dwarf's expression refused to soften as she ran her stubby finger across a piece of parchment.

"I do not." Rhoren smiled.

"Hmm." The dwarf continued to stare blankly. "What's your business with the Goldhammer Clan?"

"I was hoping to speak to Darvish about a property."

"We do tours by appointment only. Even so, I'm afraid we don't have much available at the moment, and Darvish is out of town on business for a few days. If you'd like to come back next week, we can prepare you a list of properties for rent." She sat back in her chair as if this was the end of the conversation.

Rhoren pressed forward. "Actually, I was more interested in buying than renting. I heard that there was a storefront available in the Trade District with an adjoining apartment overhead. It used to be a spice shop."

She raised her bushy red eyebrows, suddenly interested. "Oh. The, uh—"

"Cursed one." Rhoren finished her sentence with a smirk. "Let Darvish know I'm staying at the Seaside Inn when he returns."

Rhoren had the feeling he'd be hearing from Darvish very soon.

With no further business scheduled, he decided to journey down to the docks. He'd never seen the sea up close, and it would be at least several days before Darvish was back in town. Until then, he would have some fun.

The rickshaw driver dropped Rhoren off by the docks where he bought some oysters and bread from a cart vendor. Men and dwarves hauled large crates from the ships, loading them onto wagons for storage or transport. It was loud work, and seagulls lurked everywhere, picking up any scraps that might fall out.

A short stroll past the northern side of the docks led to the pier, where men fished and others sat watching the ships as they disappeared out to sea. Children played down by the shoreline, tossing shells into the water.

Rhoren walked to the end of the dock, sitting on the edge and letting his feet dangle. The waves crashed gently against the pier as he ate his bread and oysters. The oysters had been doused in vinegar, so they were a delicious mix of tangy and salty. Somehow, even the slimy texture didn't put him off. They reminded him of snails, which he'd been forced to eat on occasion. Snails tasted like dirt. These were divine.

After he finished eating, Rhoren tossed the shells into the ocean and leaned back onto his hands, letting the midday sun warm his face. He closed his eyes, listening as the waves crashed around him. Nearby, birds cawed and children laughed. Occasionally, someone would swear as their fish jumped off the line. In the distance, men yelled as they worked the docks and their hammers rang out across the waves.

Feet pattered along the dock, and Rhoren opened his eyes, surprised to see a young child sitting beside him. She held a half-eaten apple in one hand and watched him with a curious expression. The apple was brown in places, but that didn't hinder her enjoyment of it. Her curly blonde hair was windswept and speckled with sand. Bare feet dangled off the edge, her knees covered by a faded tunic splotched with saltwater.

She looked up at Rhoren with wonder. "Are you an elf?"

He laughed at the young girl's curiosity. She couldn't be more than five years old. "What gave it away?"

"James said elves have pointy ears." She pointed at Rhoren's ears. "You have pointy ears."

"That I do." Rhoren tapped the tip of his ears. "Who's James?"

"He's my brother. He brings me across the river so we can get food."

Rhoren's eyes lingered on the half-eaten apple that had more than likely been picked up off the street. "That's nice of him. What else did James tell you?"

She took a bite of her apple and the juices streamed down her chin. "He said elves live in the forest and that they don't like humans."

"I guess that depends on the elves. Some elves don't like my people either."

The young girl frowned. "There are more kinds of elves?"

The girl was curious, but she obviously wasn't well-learned in the kingdoms of Aedrea. Rhoren had been tutored by clerics ever since joining the Guard, and Charence had taken a special interest in him early on. His knowledge of the realm was on par with most noble-born. The north might be dangerous, but it was no place for idiots. Judging by the state of the girl's clothing and lack of footwear, though, she had bigger problems than schooling.

"There are two races of elves," Rhoren explained. "You have the elder elves, the oldest of the elven races. They live in the Vaglir Forest. They're tall, with blue eyes and fair skin, just like yours." He poked her arm, and she giggled. "They like to be left alone and stay with their own people. You also have the umbral elves, like me." Rhoren rolled up his sleeve. "We have dark skin, and red eyes—"

"Cindy!" An older boy's voice called out from behind them. "What are you doing? We still have work to do."

The boy wasn't much older than Cindy, maybe ten. He wore tattered and stained clothes, though he did have a pair of boots with holes in the toes. The clothing draped off his body like a scarecrow, and he was clearly underfed. His hair was shaggy blonde, and there was a weathered look to his face for someone so young.

"Look, James, I found an elf." Cindy stood with pride, pointing at Rhoren while taking another bite of her apple.

James froze in place, uncertain of what to do with this information.

Rhoren waved. "How do you do?"

James ignored the question. "Come on, Cindy. Let's go."

Cindy hurried down the dock toward James, and Rhoren called out, "Hey, are you kids hungry by chance?"

James stopped in his tracks, facing Rhoren with a look of suspicion. "What do you mean?"

Rhoren stood. "I'm new to town, and you two seem

like you know the place. If you're hungry, there's an oyster cart down the way. There's also bread and cheese. Give me some tips about the city, and I'll take care of your lunch."

James frowned, as if trying to decide if this was some kind of trick. "Fine, but we're not following you anywhere."

The kid had some smarts about him for one so young. No doubt he had been privy to some unsavory characters in his young life.

Rhoren gestured toward the docks. "Lead the way."

He followed James and Cindy across the pier, where vendors peddled their carts for those coming and going. A group of travelers unloading from a passenger ship gathered around one of the carts. James came to an abrupt stop, causing Rhoren to almost knock the boy over.

"Everything okay?" asked Rhoren.

"Actually, I think we're fine." James took a few steps back. "Nice of you to offer, but we better get going."

The kid had the panicked expression a startled animal wore just before it bolted. James looked like he couldn't afford to turn down a free meal even if he wanted, so Rhoren searched the dock for the source of the boy's distress. He found it in the form of an angry vendor stomping in their direction, leaving his cart abandoned in the street.

"Stop that boy!" the man shouted.

James grabbed Cindy by the arm and started to run, but Rhoren stepped in front of him. "Stay here. I'll handle this."

The boy's eyes darted between Rhoren and the

approaching man, and then to Cindy, who was holding onto Rhoren's pant leg.

"Behind me," he told James before returning his attention to the man.

The vendor was a portly fellow, with a large mustache that hid his lips and a sweat-stained tunic that displayed his mountain of a belly.

"You're going to pay for this, you little rats." He reached to grab James, but Rhoren swatted the man's arm away.

"Is there a problem?" Rhoren smiled as he stepped to the side, further concealing James and Cindy.

"You bet your pointy ears there's a problem." The man grunted. "This one has stolen from my cart more times than I can count. And now that I have him, I'll have his hand." He narrowed his eyes, trying to peek around Rhoren. "Let it be a lesson to the lot of them."

"What have they taken?" Rhoren asked calmly, keenly aware that at least a dozen eyes were now on him.

"What haven't they taken? I'm not sure how they do things where you're from, but theft is a crime in this city. Now hand him over so I can take him to the authorities."

The man tried to push his way past, but Rhoren's body was strong from his training in the Guard. He extended a hand, pushing the man back and nearly knocking him over.

"How dare you!" The man looked around for help, but none came. "Guards!"

Rhoren took a step forward, and the man quieted. "I will only ask you once more. If you wish to be recompensed for your missing stock, then I will require a list of the items in question. Do you really wish to punish the young for their need to survive?" Extending his blood perception, he could feel the man's racing heart pounding, his lungs expanding with each breath. Rhoren's veins writhed as he applied a small amount of pressure, and stars danced at the edge of his vision. The man coughed, suddenly having trouble breathing. He leaned forward, feeling the power within his body mounting as he whispered the rest. "Or should we continue this conversation in private?"

The man gulped as the tension released on his body. Rhoren's veins burned even from that meager display of his power, but he stood firm, waiting for the man's answer.

The man rubbed his chest, then he tallied up a list of items that he suspected James to have taken. The entire time, James stood sheepishly behind Rhoren.

When the list was complete, Rhoren paid for the stolen items, adding a few extra coins for the man's trouble. "What's your name?" Rhoren asked as he dropped the coins into the man's hand.

"Name's Dingo."

"I understand that this is your livelihood, Dingo. Make no mistake that what the boy did was wrong, but when you are fighting to survive, it is better to be wrong than starving, wouldn't you agree?" Rhoren pulled out a gold coin, holding it face-up in his palm. "If you see them hungry, and see that they eat, then this is yours."

The man puffed out his chest, eyes narrowed, then sighed. "It's easy to forget that we're all just trying to make it through the day sometimes."

With a basket full of oysters, cheese, and bread, Rhoren, James, and Cindy returned to the pier.

"Go on and take a seat, I'll be over in a minute." Rhoren handed the basket to James before slipping beneath the dock.

He braced himself against the pier and emptied his stomach into the sea. It had been months since he'd last used his abilities, and even this minor incident had taxed his body far more than he had remembered. Was it possible that his body could no longer handle the stress of using blood magic as it once had? It had been sheer determination that had kept him from passing out earlier.

Rhoren returned to find both children looking like chipmunks as they stuffed their mouths from the basket of food.

"How is it?" Rhoren sat beside James.

"Good," James muttered between bites with a full mouth.

Rhoren was content to let them finish their meal in silence, aside from the smacking jaws and grunts of pleasure. When James finished, he let out a loud belch that would make a dwarf proud.

Rhoren passed the boy his water flask and made his push for answers. "So, do either of you want to tell me why I find myself paying for your stolen food?"

"Because you're a nice elf," Cindy answered with child-like honesty.

Rhoren couldn't help but laugh. "That's kind of you, but what I mean is why have you been stealing food in the first place?"

James's shoulders fell, somewhere between shame and remorse. "We only do it when we have to."

"What do you mean?"

The boy kicked his feet out from the dock with nervous energy. "Father has our food delivered once a week, but sometimes, he's gone longer than expected. Once we run out, it's either steal or starve. We come north of the river and sometimes we find leftovers that the rich leave behind." James jumped up, as if he was about to make a run for it. "I never steal for myself, only Cindy."

Rhoren patted the aged wood for him to sit. "It's okay. I'm not here to judge you. I just want to understand. Where's your father?"

"He's on the ship." Cindy took another bite of cheese before pointing at the horizon. "He goes for long times."

"So your father is a sailor. And what about your mother?"

James rejoined them on the dock. He stared into the water as he answered. "Mother died a few years back. Father has always been a sailor, but she used to take care of us when he was gone. Now, he orders food for us, but it doesn't go far. So, we do what we have to."

Rhoren grunted. If the coin ran out and their father was gone, that was an unfortunate position indeed. The kid had done what he had to to keep his sister fed, and Rhoren respected that. Wrong and right seldom aligned with the laws of the realm.

He patted James on the knee. "Well, if you get hungry, that vendor will make sure you eat. And if he doesn't, come find me. I'll be staying at the Seaside Inn for at least a few more days. If I'm not there, the bartender, Kallum, will know where to find me." Rhoren dug in his pocket, pulling out a few silver coins. South of the river, walking around with a pocket full of gold was likely to cause two kids more problems than it could mend. "Take these, in case you need anything."

James eyed the coins suspiciously. "Why are you helping us?"

Rhoren watched as one of the ships disappeared across the horizon before answering. "I was younger than you when I lost my parents. I know how hard it is to get on without them. But this isn't a gift." He grinned. "You're going to tell me what I need to know about the city."

8. DEAL OR NO DEAL

Three days passed before Darvish showed up at the Seaside Inn. Rhoren used those three days to gather information on properties in the Trade District. City hall had been a bountiful resource, detailing how many businesses had opened in the space and how long each one had lasted. He spent an entire day sitting in the courtyard across from the empty shop, watching people come and go down the street. In the end, he felt he had enough information to make a fair offer on the property.

The emissary of the Goldhammer Clan was nearly as wide as he was tall, but he walked with an authority that had the staff and patrons moving out of his way without question. A mighty black beard draped across his chest, adorned with several engraved golden clasps. A personal guard and two attendants followed him as he entered the tavern, each one wearing the clan sigil.

Darvish looked around the tavern before settling his gaze on Kallum. "I was told there is an umbral elf staying here who wishes to speak to me."

Kallum grinned, nodding to Rhoren, who sat at the bar with a glass of white wine. "I believe this is your fellow."

Rhoren stood, extending a hand to Darvish. "Pleased to meet you."

The dwarf nodded in response, before gesturing toward a waiting table. "Please, let us talk."

The guard waited by the entryway while the two attendants sat at a nearby table. Darvish had an intense gaze as he sat down, and Rhoren expected he had used it many times when brokering deals. Lucky for Rhoren, he had stared down more fearsome foes in his time.

Without a word, the barmaid brought a platter of meats, cheeses, and bread to the table, along with a decanter for wine. A moment later, Kallum approached, holding a bottle of wine wrapped in golden foil.

Darvish licked his lips. "What do we have this time?"

Kallum smiled as he presented the bottle. The foil was pressed with the image of a single tree on top of a mountain. "Only the best for you, my good sir. This is a Rockdale red, aged seventy years."

"Seventy, you say?" Darvish frowned as if counting back the years. "Ah, yes, that was a good year indeed."

Kallum poured a small amount into the wine glass. Darvish swirled the wine and then gave it a hearty sniff, closing his eyes as he did so. Then he took a sip, making an almost slurping sound as he let it roll over his tongue.

After several nods, he spoke. "Excellent."

Kallum poured both Darvish and Rhoren a small taste, and then carefully emptied the remainder of the bottle into the decanter. "Let this breathe for a few minutes and I'll come top you off." He winked at Rhoren before returning to the bar.

Darvish took another sip of wine, this time without the theatrics. "Some say the elves have the best wine, but nothing beats an aged dwarvish red. Our cellars are the best in the realm, carved into the very mountains themselves."

Rhoren took a sip and was pleasantly surprised with how it coated his tongue. He'd tried several wines since his stay in Eastborne, but none of them were this velvety smooth. There were notes of dried figs and dark fruit, followed by hints of chocolate, nuts, and a leathery aroma.

Darvish must have noticed the surprise on Rhoren's face because he smiled for the first time. "See? Where would the world be without dwarves?"

Setting the glass on the table, Rhoren returned the smile. "My life would be a lot sadder to have never tasted such delight."

"Flattery. Now that is not something you hear from an elf every day." Darvish laughed. "Tell me, what interest do you have in my property?"

"I've come to Eastborne after a lifetime spent in the frozen north. One thing I can say about life in the Guard is that there is very little to spend your pay on." He flourished the wine, and purple waves swirled around the glass. "So here I am, ready to settle down and discover what Eastborne has to offer me."

Darvish ate a piece of bread topped with a slice of cheese, nodding along as Rhoren talked. "Why Eastborne of all places? That's an awfully long way from Cascus, and we don't get many of your kind this far south. Do you not have friends or family back home?"

Cascus was the regional name for where the umbral elf towns of Hollowton and Sanguine resided, though

Rhoren could hardly call it home. He'd spent more years in the Guard than he had in Hollowton.

"I lost my family to an attack at a young age and the Guard took me in. It's all I've ever really known."

"I'm sorry to hear that." Darvish sighed, his expression sorrowful. "Being the northernmost kingdom, Rakroft knows the value of the Northern Guard better than most. We thank you for your service."

Kallum returned to pour more of the decanted wine, but Darvish waved him away, instead choosing to stand and pour Rhoren's wine himself.

The gesture spoke volumes to Rhoren. Up north, the Guard was respected because everyone knew the dangers that lay beyond their outposts. Stories of behemoths and other monstrosities had been passed down for generations since those lands were first settled. When the Guard failed at their duty, it was these kingdoms that suffered. In the south, the Guard was more of a curiosity, something that protected the realm from threats that might or might not exist.

In the week since he'd been in Eastborne, mention of his service brought little more than contemplative looks at best. He'd lost many friends during his years in the Guard, and it was nice to see that there were those here who still honored that.

He bowed slightly to Darvish. "Thank you."

The dwarf returned to his seat after topping off his own glass. He stroked his beard and the clasps jingled against his jeweled fingers before raising his glass to Rhoren. "Now, let's talk business. Brunwilda informed me that you are looking to buy, which is why I am here in person. Dwarves are not known for our generous spirits when it comes to negotiations, and the property you've inquired about is in one of the most desired locations in the city. But in honor of your service to the realm and the history of the building, for twenty-five hundred gold, it shall be yours."

Rhoren grinned. He'd been prepared for Darvish to start the price high. Most buildings in the Trade District sold for over three thousand gold. Twenty-five hundred might be a deal, but this wasn't just any store. It was cursed, after all.

He leaned forward in his chair. "You and I both know that if this building was worth twenty-five hundred gold, it would already be sold. No one is risking their gold on a property with its reputation, not even to tear it down. You've tried renting it at a discount, but it still sits empty as often as it's filled. Every shop that has opened there over the past five years has closed within months. I sat out front for an entire day, watching the city folk as they actively avoided going anywhere near the building."

Darvish sat back in his chair, raising his brow as if taking in Rhoren in a new light. "I see you did your research."

Rhoren's lip curled at the edge. "I don't do anything in half-measures."

"A respectable quality." He placed the fingertips of both hands together. "What's your offer?"

"One thousand gold," Rhoren answered with a straight face.

Now, it was Darvish's turn to smirk. "If I let this building go for that price, the entire city would be looking to take advantage of me. Two thousand."

The offer was more than fair, but Rhoren thought he

could still do better. "This property has caused the Gold-hammer Clan headaches for years. I can make that go away. Fifteen hundred."

Darvish unleashed a boisterous laugh that carried across the tavern. "You are quite the specimen." He extended a hand. "We have ourselves a deal."

The dwarf had a surprisingly strong grip, which sent needles of pain flaring through Rhoren's wrist, a lingering effect of his adventure on the dock several days prior. Still, he couldn't help but smile. Along with his father's journal, this property was one of the few things that was truly his. He'd staked his place in the south, and for better or worse, this was his life now.

9. THE MAD HATTER

The first thing Rhoren did after acquiring the keys to his new property was remove the sign hanging from the balcony. Sugar, Spice, and Everything Nice clattered against the cobblestone as he tossed it to the street.

A door opened from the building next door, and a moment later, an older woman stood beneath the ladder. She wore a pointed hat, adorned with shimmering beads, and a silver veil that draped to her shoulders.

"What, pray tell, is the meaning of this racket?" She held a hand above her brow to block out the midday sun and placed the other on her hip.

"Ma'am." Rhoren nodded from atop the ladder. "I'm moving in upstairs and didn't want any unexpected visitors thinking this place was still in business."

"Well, just so long as you aren't banging all day long. It's bad for business." With that, she turned around and walked back inside The Mad Hatter Boutique.

Fitting name, Rhoren thought as she stormed away.

"Don't mind Helena," a gravelly voice called from a few

buildings down, where a gruff-looking man leaned against a lamp post smoking a pipe. "She's got a lot of bark in her, but she doesn't bite."

The man walked over, a steady stream of smoke following him as he puffed. He was broad-shouldered, with an unkempt beard that sprouted from his face in all directions. His bright blue eyes stood out prominently from his weathered face. The ruggedness of his appearance contrasted with his well-tailored tunic, polished boots, and fine pants.

"Name's Titus." He pulled the pipe from his lips and saluted it in Rhoren's direction. "You're a braver elf than most to try your luck with this place. What business are you in?"

Rhoren climbed down the ladder, introducing himself and shaking the man's hand. "No business. I just wanted the apartment upstairs."

"Interesting." Titus raised an eyebrow. "Like I said, Helena loves to cause a fuss if there's ever an occasion, but pay her no mind and she'll leave you be eventually." He took a step back, gesturing up the street with his pipe. "I'm a glover myself. The wife and I run a shop up the way called Glove Yourself. Her name, not mine." He chuckled. "Anyways, I'll leave you to it."

"Thanks for the warning." Rhoren grinned. "I'll make sure to stop by if I'm ever in need of new gloves."

With the sign gone, Rhoren stepped into his new home. The interior was the same as it had been the previous week when he first peered through the window. Dust covered everything aside from a few trails where some creature had certainly found their way inside.

A few empty vials and bottles littered the floor, but in

one corner, an unopened bottle had been left behind. Rhoren wiped the dust from the label, revealing a picture of a leaf with a flame to one side and a snowflake to the other.

Fire and Ice Basil.

On the back, there was a hand-written description.

This rare spice amplifies the peppery and minty flavors of traditional basil to give any recipe a spark of deliciousness.

The bottle contained close to a dozen dried leaves. It sounded like an interesting ingredient, but he couldn't imagine a great need for such a product when fresh basil was already easily accessible at the market. Then again, he was living in a different world now, where people spent gold like it was going out of style.

The ground floor was a decent enough size for a shop, with plenty of room for shelves and cabinets. He could hardly imagine filling the entire space with special spices, but his knowledge of high-end spices was limited to the bottle in his hand.

Upstairs, the apartment was better than he imagined. Though it was covered in a layer of dust, he could already envision filling it with furniture. The second floor consisted of a single large room, which Darvish had referred to as a flat, with a small kitchen, a bathroom, a fireplace, and a nook for storage. It was the same square footage as the floor below, except instead of a porch out front, it had a balcony that overlooked the square.

Rhoren opened the door to the balcony and let fresh air flow into the room, sending dust bunnies tumbling toward the kitchen. Cleaning would be his first order of business, and he could spend a few more days at the Seaside Inn while he sorted this place out.

He took a moment to appreciate the view. At the edge of the square, he could see across the tiered city, all the way down to the harbor where ships speckled the sea.

After a quick trip to the general store, Rhoren returned with a broom, cleaning rags, a mop, and a bucket. During his early days in the Guard, before his skills were deemed sufficient to travel into the wilderness, cleaning had been a part of his duties. The same as every other new recruit.

He could have paid someone to come and clean the place, but there was a certain satisfaction in doing it himself, as mundane as the task may seem.

As he swept through the dirt and dust, those memories came flooding back. After the attack in Hollowton, he'd been lost, but he soon found that he wasn't alone. As the months had passed, he'd found himself a part of two brotherhoods—the Northern Guard as a whole, but also the Order of Blood Mages.

In the north, politics came second to survival. The Guard's loyalty was to the realm of Aedrea as a whole, not to any particular kingdom, region, or race. He'd made friends and fought alongside his brothers and sisters, celebrating their victories and mourning their defeats.

Rhoren's mind continued to wander as the pile of dust grew larger.

Even though the umbral elves made up a fraction of the Guard's members, they somehow produced more blood mages per capita than any other race. Perhaps it was part of the price his people had paid long ago to rid the world of elven immortality.

Humans and dwarves made up the majority of the Guard, while gnomes and halflings were as few as the umbral elves with only a handful of elder elves among their ranks. He'd often wondered if elder elves produced blood mages at a similar rate and kept them hidden away within the depths of their forests. As secretive as they were, he wouldn't put it past them.

None of that mattered now, though. He was far away from that life, and judging by the way his body still ached after his last use of magic, he was never going back. He flexed his fingers, and pinpricks spiked throughout, less than the day before but still uncomfortable. In the days since he'd arrived in Eastborne, his pain had been steadily decreasing. All it took was a moment to erase that progress.

He'd be more careful going forward.

With the top floor swept and cobwebs dusted, Rhoren stood back, taking in the bare bones of his new home. He pressed his hand to the wall, feeling the cool stone against his palm. This would do just fine.

There was a fullness within him that he hadn't felt in quite some time. Comfort, or perhaps simply a calmness compared to his life in the Guard? Whatever it was, he didn't want to let it go.

10. COGWALLOPER

"Another one?" Kallum held the wine bottle at an angle over Rhoren's glass.

Rhoren nodded, and Kallum topped off the glass with more of the golden wine. The umbral elf had become an evening regular whenever Kallum was bartending. Even after moving into his new place, he'd still found himself coming back night after night to chat with the bearded man. Kallum was easy to talk to and he'd yet to make a bad drink.

Kallum set the bottle on the bar with the label facing Rhoren—a bear with a paw reaching into a honey pot. "How's the new place treating you? No more run-ins with the Mad Hatter?"

Rhoren laughed. "As long as I keep the noise down, she leaves me be. I admire her spirit, though."

Kallum raised a brow. "You're likely the only one. She's a shrew if I ever saw one."

Rhoren sipped his wine. The white wine from Whit-blossom was unique in its taste, more herbaceous than the other white wines he had sampled. There were notes of green pepper followed by a refreshing aftertaste of juicy white peach.

The more he'd tried various wines over the last few weeks, the easier it became to describe the nuance of aroma and tasting notes. Like a painter discovering new hues and shades, his palette broadened. Instead of saying something tasted fruity, he began to understand the flavor profiles of a variety of fruits from green apple to grapefruit and blood orange. Kallum would explain how the wine tasted to him, occasionally providing a sample from the kitchen for the flavors Rhoren wasn't familiar with. His knowledge grew with each passing day.

As he sat there enjoying this newest wine, Rhoren opened his father's journal while Kallum chatted with another guest at the end of the bar. His increasing knowledge of taste and flavor opened new interpretations of his father's descriptions.

The cucumber adds a refreshing component to contrast the sweetness of the berries. A floral-tasting jin is recommended, but others can bring about a more citrusy experience.

This past week was the first time Rhoren had ever tasted a cucumber, one of the key ingredients in the Berry Cucumber Revival.

"Is that where you keep all your deep, dark secrets?" Kallum smirked as he gestured at the journal, pulling Rhoren from his reading. "I swear you carry that book everywhere you go."

Rhoren set the journal on the bar, tapping the cover. "This belonged to my father. It's a collection of recipes from his travels."

"Recipes? Your father was a cook?" Kallum crafted a

cocktail as he spoke, muddling a cube of sugar into the bottom of a glass.

"Not quite. He had an appreciation for cocktails." Rhoren opened the journal, showing Kallum some of its contents. "There are a few dozen recipes in here. Each one lists the ingredients, tasting notes, where he learned it from, and usually a few other details."

"How are you just now telling me this?" Kallum stopped shaking the drink and leaned forward for a better look. "By the gods, Rhoren, this is amazing! You and I are about to have a long talk about withholding secrets from friends."

"Friends?" Rhoren grinned. "Is that what we are now?"

Kallum strained the drink into a glass and topped it with a cherry. "That will greatly depend on whether or not you let me peruse that journal of yours." He winked as he left to deliver the cocktail.

Rhoren wasn't sure why he hadn't shared his father's journal with Kallum already. The two had become friendly enough. Based on the reaction of the bartender in Hollowton when he saw the contents, he knew that Kallum would enjoy it just as much, but something had caused him to hold back.

Maybe it was because sharing an item from his past would invite more questions into his own life. Questions he wasn't ready to answer. Talking about his father would inevitably lead to discussing his death. As far as Kallum knew, Rhoren was a member of the Northern Guard, a hardworking soldier who had earned his retirement. It was more of a half-truth than a complete lie. He'd just left out the part about being a blood mage and one of the most powerful magic-wielders in the realm.

What did it matter anyways? Aside from the incident on the dock, which he had achingly paid for, Rhoren's powers were a thing of the past.

When Kallum returned, Rhoren opened the journal and set it facing the bartender. "Here, have a look."

Kallum's eyes widened as he turned the pages. "This is exquisite detail. He recorded everything. Ingredients, tasting notes, appearance, presentation, and history of the drink. This should be required reading for any serious bartender." He shook his head in awe. "You'll have to introduce me if he ever visits."

Rhoren's cheeks flushed, suddenly filled with heat. "He passed away when I was a child. This is the only thing I have of his."

Kallum's smile faded, and he closed the journal, handing it back to Rhoren. "I'm sorry. I didn't know."

"It's fine." Rhoren held up a hand, refusing to accept the journal. "I've always wanted to try some of the recipes. So far, I've only managed one." His eyes locked with Kallum's. "Would you mind?"

"It would be an honor." Kallum opened the journal once again, this time holding it like some priceless artifact. Every flip of the page was so delicate, as if too much force might turn the paper to ash. "Do you have a preference?"

Rhoren winked. "Surprise me."

Kallum worked with the finesse of a great painter, carefully measuring ingredients into what Rhoren had learned was a shaker. The shaker was nothing more than two metal containers in the shape of a glass, one large and one small that fit snugly together in order to mix ingredients.

After adding a spoonful of red syrup, several squeezes of lime, and a handful of ice chips from the chiller, Kallum shook the shaker vigorously until a cool sheen covered the outside. Then he strained a small amount into a glass to taste. Happy with the result, he strained the remainder of the liquid into a coupe glass, dropping three raspberries into the bright red drink and garnishing the rim with a wedge of lime.

With a mischievous smile, Kallum placed the drink in front of Rhoren.

"What do we have here?" Rhoren asked as he admired the cocktail from different angles.

"Try it first, then I'll tell you."

Rhoren lifted the glass and sniffed. The strong whiff of alcohol overtook the scent of raspberry and lime. Contrary to its fruity appearance, this was not a drink for lightweights. He tilted the glass, letting the cool drink linger on his tongue before swallowing. It was refreshing, semi-sweet, and surprisingly tart, with a warmth that trailed down into his stomach. Even though it was strong, the alcohol was well hidden. This was a dangerous drink.

"Well?" Kallum watched him expectantly.

"It's wonderful." He took another sip. "So, what is it?"

"The Cogwalloper." Kallum laughed as he turned the journal around, pointing to the description of the drink where Rhoren's father had even sketched a picture of the coupe glass. "Your father left quite an entertaining description on that one."

Rhoren grinned as he recalled the imagery of gnomish thugs before reading it again.

Cogwalloper

Ingredients:

2.5 oz Gold Rhum
.5 oz Raspberry Syrup
.5 oz Lime Juice
.25 oz Orange Liqueur

Beneath the ingredient list and instructions, there was a sketch of the drink, complete with a lime wedge, followed by more notes.

Taste: *Sweet and refreshing. Fruit-forward, and slightly tart. Dangerously boozy.*

Appearance: *Deep reddish color. The color varies based on the potency of the raspberry syrup. The longer the syrup sits, the more enriched it will become. Garnished with a raspberry float, lime wedge, or both.*

I learned of the Cogwalloper during my travels through the gnomish lands of Revelia. The bartender at the Gooseberry Pub, Manlin, told me that the drink owed its origins to the seedy underbelly of the city of Cogwall. The enforcers of the underground clans were known as Cogwallopers for the overzealous beatings they dealt toward anyone who ran afoul of the so-called "clan business." The gnomes had a fondness for drinks both strong and fruity, and this one delivers on both counts.

"He really had a way with words." Rhoren traced a finger over the long-dried ink. "You've done him proud."

"That's very kind of you." Kallum closed the journal and placed it next to Rhoren. "Perhaps I can try out some more of your father's recipes in the future."

Maybe it was the alcohol talking, but Rhoren thought that he'd found his first true friend since leaving the Guard. He rested his hand on the journal before looking up at Kallum. "I can't think of anyone better."

The tavern slowly filled, and as the night wore on, Kallum was busied with drink orders and bottle service. Rhoren took his drink and found a place on the patio balcony overlooking the sea. Seagulls swooped in the moonlight, and stars twinkled across the endless dark blue water while Rhoren sipped his Cogwalloper in peace.

11. BUMP IN THE NIGHT

Rhoren woke with a start. There was a thud and then a grating sound from the floor below. He was alert in an instant, fighting against years of training to use his blood sense at the first sign of disturbance. The habit was so ingrained in him that it had become second nature when traveling beyond the outposts. Scanning the area for beating hearts had saved the lives of him and his men on more than one occasion during their ventures into the northern wilderness.

He took a deep breath and let the tingling sensation fade from his hands. There were no behemoths here, nothing worth setting back his recovery yet again.

With the skill of a rogue, Rhoren crept down the stairs. Moonlight shone through the front windows, casting a silver glow on the empty room. Outside, a member of the city watch marched past as they patrolled the streets.

As he looked around, nothing seemed out of place, not that there was much to begin with. The doors were locked, the windows intact. Perhaps, some creature had found its way underneath the floorboards or between the walls.

Or maybe this old building just liked to talk. Creaky floors and shifts in the foundation were more likely than evil spirits trying to scare him away.

He chuckled as he sat on the bottom stair, remembering Jesper's fear of wraiths, specters, and shadow fairies.

Shadow fairies were mischievous creatures, but they dwelled in the depths of forests. If they were in the city, then they most certainly wouldn't stick to one building.

Specters were a possibility, but there'd been nothing to indicate tragedy had befallen any of the former occupants of the building, not with those he'd interviewed or in the records at city hall. Maybe something had happened before official record-keeping began, but it seemed unlikely. If ghastly spirits were roaming the streets of Eastborne, someone would have seen something. Rhoren had only heard of specters haunting ruins where some great tragedy had happened. One of the Guard's abandoned outposts was haunted by the specters of dead soldiers.

Wraiths were out of the question entirely. If there was a wraith in the city, there would be a trail of bodies and an army of clerics ready to send it to the great beyond.

Rhoren's hair stood on end as he recalled the only time he'd encountered a wraith while in the Guard. It had taken a light mage and a dozen clerics a full day to destroy the enraged spirit. The scene still haunted him.

They were dangerous apparitions, formed of vitriol and hate. Being incorporeal, they were also immune to blood magic. When a specter absorbed too much dark emotion, it became a wraith, completely controlled by its shadowy nature. Wraiths were vile revenants capable of draining the essence of anyone within their vicinity. Left unchecked, they could devour entire towns.

Something had certainly scared the shop owners away from this building, but whatever it was hadn't tried to hurt them.

Rhoren leaned back against the stairwell, admiring the beauty of the building in the moonlight. The place had good bones—a tall ceiling with exposed beams, an elegant fireplace, sturdy walls, and well-maintained floorboards. It seemed wrong to leave such a space empty. The problem was that Rhoren's skills as a blood mage didn't exactly translate to civilian life. He had no great talents or specialized knowledge. He wasn't industrious or business savvy. All he had was a lot of free time and a decently sized savings. The rest and relaxation were nice, and his body felt better than it had in years, but eventually, he'd want more.

But what?

Kallum had hit the nail on the head when he'd said Rhoren lacked purpose.

He sighed, leaning forward until his elbows rested on his knees. What good was a life without meaning?

A piece of debris fell in the fireplace, disturbed by some bat or owl that had made its chimney home. Maybe that had been the source of the noise.

He stood, examining the fireplace. Structurally, it was the focal point of the ground floor, with its massive hearth and imposing mantle. It likely hadn't been used often by the former shop owners, but it was a magnificent piece worthy of tall tales and hearty drinks.

Rhoren clapped his hands as he suddenly envisioned the space in a new light. It wasn't as big as the Seaside Inn, not by a long shot, but it might be just big enough. Slowly, the building began to take shape in his mind's eye. A large bar along the right wall with shelves for bottles and glasses, several tables in the back, and a few oversized chairs around the fireplace. It wouldn't do for your run-of-the-mill tavern where drinks were cheap and patrons were rowdy, but for a place that served specialized drinks that were worth the price...

If he could bring his father's drinks to life, breaking even would be more than enough.

12. ORANGE FIZZ

Rhoren sat on his balcony, enjoying a cup of peppermint tea as the city stirred to life around him. Birds chirped in the early morning air, and the streets were full of chatter as people began their day. It was vastly different from up north, where training started early. Grunts, curses, and the clash of steel had been his norm for so long. Nowadays, mornings were for tea and rumination.

And people-watching.

He took another sip of the fragrant tea, observing the city folk as they scurried around like mice in the woods. Watching his neighbors in the throes of life had become one of his favorite ways to pass the time. Somehow, it had added a new perspective to his time served in the Guard. Down below, people rushed about, the problems of their mundane lives front and center. For most of them, their worldview expanded no further than the city walls.

They paid no price for their peace and had no idea how lucky they truly were.

Rhoren's rumination came to an abrupt halt when he

spotted Kallum walking across the square toward his apartment.

The man's silver beard was a sight to behold and hard to ignore even in a sea of people. Rhoren often wondered how much care it required to tame such a magnificent beast. Kallum carried a wicker basket in one hand and a knapsack over his shoulder, whistling as he walked. When he saw Rhoren, Kallum tossed up a hand in greeting.

"Morning!"

Rhoren stood, nearly spilling his tea at this unexpected appearance. "Morning! What are you doing out this way so early?"

"I have the day off." He lifted the basket. "Thought I would be a good neighbor and show you one of Eastborne's best-kept secrets."

"Is that so?" Rhoren raised a brow. "I'd hate to be the one to hinder your good deeds. I'll be down in a moment."

He did his best to conceal his excitement as he dressed. He enjoyed Kallum's company, and this would be the first time the two of them had spent time together outside of the inn. It was one thing to claim friendship as Rhoren bought drinks and tipped generously, but it was quite another to seek him out on his day off.

Rhoren couldn't help but wonder what the man had in store.

"I'm assuming you know how to ride a horse?" Kallum asked as he led them through the city.

Rhoren nodded as he searched for clues regarding their destination. Kallum refused to reveal the contents of his basket or divulge any information as they continued through Eastborne's lower tiers, adding to the intrigue.

After securing two horses from someone Kallum kept

referring to as a "good friend," they passed through the northern gates. They traveled along the coast until the noise from the docks disappeared entirely. The horses were well-trained and made for an easy ride as the stone streets eventually turned to dirt. Occasionally, they passed a carriage or cart heading toward Eastborne, but the road was mostly empty.

Rhoren found himself transfixed as waves crashed against the shore. There was a peacefulness that abounded in nature, far from the sounds of cities and towns. He often found that peace up north as he and his men trudged through the snow on their missions, when conversation had worn dry and all that was left was the crunch of snow beneath their boots.

He took a deep breath as the horses trotted along, inhaling the salty air, and finding gratitude that his days of fighting behemoths were at an end.

The sun was high overhead before Kallum stopped for a break. The man grimaced as he climbed down from the horse, walking with a slight exaggeration to his step. "Well, don't you look fresh as a daisy?" Kallum frowned as he rubbed his backside. "They should really make these things more comfortable."

"You should have asked your special friend for a carriage." Rhoren grinned. "Sure you don't want me to carry that basket for a bit?"

Kallum tapped the top of the basket. "You just want to know what's inside."

"You're guarding the contents like it's some priceless artifact. Can you blame me?"

Kallum laughed. "I suppose not. But don't worry, we're nearly there." He pointed ahead toward a bend, where the road curved to the left, and a copse of trees blocked the view of the sea. "We'll take the last bit on foot."

They walked the horses the rest of the way, where beyond the trees a small peninsula jutted into the sea. A sandy trail led down the strip of land to a rocky formation where a single tree had managed to stake its claim between the rocks. It swayed gently in the breeze.

Kallum tied both horses to a tree, and gestured toward the peninsula. "After you."

Once they were out there, the trees concealed the roads and all signs of civilization, and the horses grazed happily on the untouched grass. It was like they were on a deserted island with nothing more than the contents of Kallum's mysterious basket and satchel.

"What is this place?" Rhoren asked as he stared out at the sea.

Kallum set the basket on a formation of rocks as flat as a table. "They call it Pondering Pointe. Many scholars and clerics have come here over the years in search of enlightenment."

"I can see why." Rhoren's mind drifted for a moment to his conversation with Charence. The cleric had said many in his order believed they were entering a new age of enlightenment abandoned by the gods. "It's very peaceful."

"It's a good place to reset." Kallum stood beside Rhoren, taking a deep breath and closing his eyes. "The city is great, but it can be a little much at times. Every once in a while, I just need to escape."

Rhoren understood the sentiment. There were times in his life before when he wanted to run away, but his sense of duty always kept him honest.

He sat on one of the rocks and nodded toward the

basket. "When do we get to see what surprises you brought?"

"You're worse than a child." Kallum grinned as he sat, lifting the lid to the basket. "Don't get too excited. The real treat was coming here, but I brought some food and a special drink. Consider it a thank you for letting me read your father's journal."

Kallum placed a piece of checkered cloth across the timeworn stone, meticulously pressing the creases and edges until it lay flat. Then he removed several items, each one wrapped in waxed paper and knotted with twine. Every movement was delicate as he untied the twine bows, revealing an assortment of cheeses and meats. Next, he pulled out a loaf of bread, a jar of honey, and an assortment of fruits.

Rhoren's mouth watered at the spread before him. "You really are a master of presentation."

The display was so elegant that it wouldn't look out of place on a table at the Seaside Inn.

"I guess you're not the only one who doesn't do anything in half-measures." He smirked.

Rhoren furrowed his brow in mock outrage. "Is it bad taste for bartenders to eavesdrop on guest conversations?"

"Bad taste? It's practically inn policy. Everyone knows bartenders have the best gossip." He reached into the basket and pulled out two wine glasses wrapped in a thick layer of cloth that had protected them within the basket. "Hold these. I think you'll appreciate this part."

Kallum pulled out a bottle of orange juice, careful not to spill any as he filled each glass halfway. Then, with the practiced motion of someone who had presented a wine bottle hundreds, if not thousands, of times, he revealed a sparkling wine to Rhoren.

"Orange juice and sparkling wine?" Rhoren gave him a questioning look. They seemed like two things that didn't belong together.

"I call it an Orange Fizz. Equal parts sparkling wine and freshly-squeezed juice. Well, freshly squeezed this morning." After popping the cork, he filled the glasses the rest of the way with wine until the bubbles threatened to overflow. "To new friends and much-needed escapes."

Rhoren clinked his glass against Kallum's. "Cheers to that."

The orange and sparkling wine played off of one another in a refreshing twist that somehow made both taste better than they did alone. He'd been wrong to ever question Kallum's abilities as a bartender.

As they sat there enjoying the sunny day, Kallum suddenly jumped to his feet, pointing out to sea. "Look at that! Sea unicorns!"

Far out at sea, a pod of shimmering white sea creatures moved across the horizon, each one with a long opalescent horn protruding from the top of its head. They dove through the air in magnificent arcs, leaving a rainbow mist in their wake.

"You must be good luck. I've been coming here for years and never seen one." Kallum kept his eyes fixated on the sea unicorns as they continued their journey.

"Or maybe it was the Orange Fizz," Rhoren teased. "They are beautiful, though. Majestic creatures. I'd heard that unicorns lived within the depths of the wilds. Are these known for their healing as well?"

Unicorns were revered across Aedrea for their incredible healing properties. Some of the most expensive elixirs and potions were made using unicorn ingredients. They could cure poisons and treat fatal sicknesses, but they did little against the effects caused by casting blood magic.

Kallum shrugged. "I don't know. No captain would risk his crew to find out, either. They say to kill a sea unicorn is to never sail again, that killing something so pure provokes the wrath of the kraken."

"The kraken? Those things actually exist?" They sounded more like myths than actual monsters, but if behemoths and dragons existed, why not the terror of the seas? If what he'd heard was true, their size dwarfed behemoths.

"I've heard tales of ships that were swallowed whole by the kraken. I appreciate the beauty of the sea as well as the next man, but you'll never catch me on a ship." The sea unicorns finally vanished from sight, and Kallum returned his attention to the food, tossing a grape in his mouth. "But I'm sure you've seen your share of terrors in the Guard, if the stories are true."

The Orange Fizz began to take effect, and Rhoren leaned against the rocks to steady himself. "What stories are those?"

"The terrors of the north. Direbears. Ice dragons. Behemoths. I'm sure there are more I'm not familiar with. They say that behemoth hides are impervious to arcane magic, and that it would take a hundred men to bring one down. That if not for the blood mages, they would roam freely across the lands destroying anything in their path."

Rhoren could feel Kallum's lingering gaze as he stared out at the sea. "They're real, alright. The most terrifying beings I've ever set my eyes on."

"More terrifying than the blood mages?" asked Kallum.

Rhoren nearly dropped his glass at the unexpected question. "What do you mean?"

"I've met arcane mages before. Working in the Noble District, we see them coming and going from time to time. Sure, they're pompous and think awfully high of themselves, but they have rules of conduct and hold each other accountable. But the blood mages, I have to imagine there's something unsettling about being near someone who could stop your heart from beating just by looking at you. Don't you agree?"

Rhoren sat in silence for a long moment. Was this how people viewed him in the south? As someone more terrifying than the monsters he fought to protect them from. Up north, there were songs written in honor of the blood mages. The Guard was respected. But here—

Kallum tapped him on the leg. "You okay?"

"Sorry, it's just that I've seen the monsters in the north. I've witnessed their power, and I've fought beside good men who died facing down those monsters. Good blood mages, too. Do you know the pain it causes a blood mage to call on their power, the toll it takes on the body and mind to endure that day in and day out? Blood mages don't choose their powers and most wish that they'd never discovered them to begin with. For a blood mage to join the Northern Guard is to stare down death, and to welcome it if it comes. I see nothing unsettling about that."

He wasn't sure why he lied. Or if what he'd said truly was a lie. A lie by omission, perhaps. Maybe it was the fear of Kallum's response, or the worry of losing the only friend he'd made in the city over something that didn't matter anymore. There were no behemoths in Eastborne. If his powers faded into the ether no one would be the wiser.

"Gods, I'm a prick." Kallum buried his head in his palm. "Obviously, I know nothing of the north or the blood mages. Or the Guard for that matter. You've lived that life, and I'm sorry I was so insensitive. I should be asking questions, not making assumptions."

That eased Rhoren's worry slightly, but he let his lie hold. This was a new beginning for him. No one had to know about his life before.

He patted Kallum on the back. "Don't worry about it. It's like you said, the troubles of the north hardly matter here. As long as that holds true, the Guard is doing its job." He mixed himself another drink and attempted to change the subject to brighter topics. "Speaking of questions. What made you want to become a bartender?"

Kallum tilted back the glass, draining the rest of his drink. "My family owns a tavern in Tiberia. But with four brothers and three sisters, I wanted to find my own way in the world. So, I moved to Eastborne at fifteen, working in one of the more sketchy taverns south of the river. I have some stories I could tell from those days, believe me. With each new job, I learned a little more, eventually working my way across the river and into better districts. I've been at the Seaside Inn for almost a decade now."

"And you're happy?"

Kallum laughed. "Don't let my outburst from the other day fool you. I love my job. I love the opportunities it brings and the lifestyle it allows me to live. Half the tavern owners in the city would close up shop for my job in a heartbeat. I don't have to be the boss to be content."

"What if you could be?"

"What if I could be what?" Kallum wore a puzzled expression.

"What if you could be the boss?"

His eyes narrowed. "What are you getting at, Rhoren?"

Rhoren wasn't sure if Kallum was intrigued or annoyed, but he pressed on anyway. "It could be a terrible idea, but I've been tossing it around in the back of my mind and can't seem to let it go. I've got this empty storefront, and my father's journal. You've said it yourself how amazing his recipes are. Maybe that could be my new purpose. But I don't know the first thing about running a tavern and know even less about bartending. I thought that if you were up to it, maybe we could build it up together. Half of the recipes are yours; half would be my father's. What do you think?"

The silence hung in the air for so long that Rhoren was about to rescind the offer. Asking someone he'd known for only a couple of weeks to give up a respectable job and open a new tavern probably wasn't the wisest choice to begin with.

Kallum burst out laughing. "Oh, it's definitely a terrible idea, and considering the history of the building, it might be cursed from the start." He grinned and his blue eyes were full of excitement. "But it might be fun."

Rhoren smirked. "You worry about the cocktails. Leave the curses to me."

Kallum extended a hand. "Deal."

13. GOOD BONES

Converting the storefront into a tavern worthy of its location wouldn't be easy. More-so, it wouldn't be cheap. The cost of building materials, permits, and high-end spirits would add up fast, which was why Rhoren found himself at the Bank of Aedrea.

There were local and regional banks all across the realm, but the Bank of Aedrea was the only one that operated within every kingdom. It also happened to be where the Northern Guard held its funds. Being that the Guard had no industry or source of income, it was funded by each of the nine kingdoms.

The bank was operated by the Order of Clerics, and therefore had good standing across the realm. It was hard for anyone, king or not, to argue with the will of the gods. With a cleric in almost every town, the order had more influence and information than any single kingdom. So, it was no surprise that they already knew of Rhoren's relocation.

The halfling clerk slid a piece of parchment detailing

Rhoren's account balance across the counter. "Charence said we'd be seeing you soon. He speaks very highly of you, Bloodbane."

Rhoren looked over his shoulder to make sure no one had heard his mage name before leaning forward. "Please, call me Rhoren. I'd rather not everyone know where I come from."

"Noted." The halfling scribbled a note on a piece of paper. "I will make sure it doesn't happen again. Your pension will be deposited on the first of the month. We appreciate your service to the realm and look forward to doing business with you."

Rhoren folded the parchment and stashed it in his pocket. He and Kallum hadn't discussed the proposition any further since their adventure outside of the city, but they were scheduled to meet later this afternoon to go over some of the details. Rhoren had a good amount of savings, but he expected to put a hefty dent into it over the coming weeks. Eastborne wasn't a cheap city to begin with, and owning property in the Trade District came with its own expectations.

Even though nothing had been set in motion yet, it was practically all he had thought about since their picnic.

That wasn't entirely true. The mysterious noises had awakened him on several occasions. There was no rhyme or reason to them. Sometimes a loud thud; other times, incessant scratching. He was certain the noises were coming from some creature, but without using his abilities, he hadn't been able to locate the source of the disturbance.

He would put an end to it soon enough, starting by filling the downstairs with rodent traps. If something was sneaking in at night, this would put an end to it. He was determined to solve the issue without his blood magic.

After leaving the bank, Rhoren went to the general store, where he found a hearty supply of traps. The cashier was a skeletal man, his face gaunt and sunken, but he was nice enough to offer instruction on how to set the traps. He assured Rhoren that whatever he was dealing with, it was nothing compared to the rats south of the river.

The man placed the trap on the counter and pried back the hammer, the metal rod that would spell the doom of the intruding creature, latching it in place with a click. "What you want to do is find something to bait the rodent, a piece of cheese or bread. Really lure them in. When they try to take the bait, it will activate the trap, and the hammer will come down. Splat!" He grinned devilishly. "You can clean off the blood and entrails and reuse it as much as you need. If it turns out you're dealing with something bigger, I'd recommend you see the alchemists. South of the river, the rats are as big as cats! Only way to kill 'em is with poison. It'll cost more, but it'll get the job done."

"I'll keep that in mind." Rhoren stuffed the traps in his bag. Hopefully, he'd have the problem fixed by the end of the week without the need for poison.

Back home, he'd barely finished placing his new purchases when someone knocked at the door. Kallum grinned as he waved from outside the window.

Rhoren opened the door, squeezing Kallum on the arm as he invited him inside for the first time. "I've been looking forward to this all week."

"Me too!" Kallum's foot tapped against a trap set by the

door, and it activated with a loud clack. He raised a brow. "What's going on here?"

Rhoren looked at the ground sheepishly. "Nothing to worry about. Just making preparations for any unwanted visitors."

Kallum slid the trap against the wall with his foot. "So you think it was rats that sent the last occupants packing?"

Rhoren ran his fingers through his hair and dark strands fell to one side. "I don't know what it was that scared them away, but I'm sure the only spirits in here are the ones we'll be serving."

"Alright, soldier. I'll leave you to wage war against the rodents." Kallum grinned. "Now tell me, what did you have in mind for this place?"

Rhoren's hands tingled with excitement as he darted around the room, using his hands to showcase the layout he envisioned. "The fireplace is gorgeous. I think it would be a crime not to make it the focal point. We could put the bar along this wall, some tables in the back and maybe a few more out on the porch if the neighbors don't mind. We don't want a rowdy tavern where people are throwing each other out the door. I say we make it cozy and refined, a place that's worthy of the high-quality drinks we would offer."

"I like that." Kallum walked around the room as if he was seeing it all play out before him. "Haunted or not, you really lucked out with this place. It's a sound structure. Good bones. Whoever built it put in the hard work." He pointed to the wall over the fireplace. "A few tapestries along the wall would liven the place up and really show-case the structure. And maybe a chandelier in the center to catch the light of the fire. Oh, and a raised platform at the back for musicians."

Rhoren stood with his arms crossed, grinning.

"What?" asked Kallum.

"It's a good feeling."

"What's that?" Kallum arched a brow.

"I don't know if I've ever had this kind of excitement for something. I've had purpose. I've had duty. But this, this is different. I can feel it in my core."

"Good." Kallum returned his smile. "This is going to take a lot of work, but if we do it right, I think we can really make something of this place."

"Alright, alright. Let's get down to business."

They sat on the balcony upstairs, which Rhoren had furnished with a small table and two chairs. The early afternoon sun kissed their skin as Rhoren placed a quill and ink on the table next to his father's journal and some blank sheets of parchment.

He took a deep breath, his chest suddenly tight. This was it. Their first real discussion on what this place could be.

"Where do we begin?" Rhoren pinched his brow, trying to ease some of the tension. "I don't know the first thing about starting a business, so do you want to take the lead?"

Kallum must have sensed Rhoren's worry, because he grabbed the elf's hand and squeezed. "We'll take it one step at a time." He let go of Rhoren's hand and smiled, pulling a leather notebook from his bag. "Don't worry. I came prepared."

Of course he had. Kallum's attention to detail was one of the things Rhoren appreciated most about the man.

Kallum opened the notebook. "I think we should handle things in the most logical order. Obviously, getting the layout of the building and constructing a bar, tables, and whatever else we need is the priority. Working at one of the premier inns in Eastborne has its perks. I know a few builders that should give us a decent price. We'll need to settle on decor as well. We can make a day of visiting some of the shops to find tapestries and whatever else we might want. Glassware, as well as the spirits we stock, will depend on the drinks we're serving, but I think it will be good to have a variety of wines as well as a few kegs that we keep on a seasonal rotation. What do you think?"

Rhoren nodded. "That all sounds good to me."

"Good, I think it will be best to keep our inventory small starting out. A few of your father's drinks and a few of mine. Once we build up some clientele, then we can start expanding the menu and double down on what sells the best. One thing I'd considered was food. People love to eat when they drink, even if it's something small. I'm not sure what we would do about that since there's not room for a kitchen."

"Actually..." Rhoren wagged a finger as he sat forward. "I've considered that myself, and I think I may have a solution."

"Really?" Kallum rubbed his hands together. "Let's hear it."

"What if we had food carts set up outside the building? A different one each night. In exchange for a small percentage of their profits, we would provide them with steady business."

Kallum stood up so fast that his chair slid several

inches across the balcony. "Rhoren, that's bloody brilliant! How has no one thought of that before?"

"Oh, I'm sure someone has. It's not exactly inventing the wheel."

"So modest." Kallum frowned. "Most taverns are built with the intention of selling drinks and food. The kitchen is part of the building. Sure, some vendors lurk outside of taverns trying to catch the stray offerings here and there, but I don't know of anyone who has partnered with food peddlers for business. With an idea like that, you could open a tavern in any building across Eastborne without the need for a kitchen. It's a brilliant idea."

Rhoren's cheeks grew hot at the abundant praise. It had seemed like a simple solution to the lack of space. "I'll start reaching out to some of the street vendors later in the week. How soon do you think we can have the builders ready?"

"I'll check in with a few before my shift tomorrow." Kallum bit his lip. "Can I ask you something?"

"What is it?"

"How do you plan on paying for all of this? It's none of my business. Well, I guess maybe some of it's my business if we're doing this together... But what I mean is, opening a business is a risky endeavor. You just retired, and as much as I want this to succeed, I'd hate for you to take out a loan and then the business go belly-up."

"Don't worry about that. I've been saving since I joined the Guard. I have enough to get us started. After that—" He laughed. "—let's just say I pray my father's drinks are as good as we think they are."

"There's not a doubt in my mind about that." Kallum sighed as he looked out over the square. "I'm not looking forward to breaking the news to Timofey. He's never been good at taking bad news."

Rhoren grimaced. "I do not envy that conversation."

"Best to get it over with. It'll be worse if he finds out from some loose-lipped builder that I've been slinking around town behind his back." He looked Rhoren in the eye. "We're really doing this?"

Rhoren took a deep breath. For the first time in his life, he was given a say in how his future unfolded. Whether it was the will of the gods or blind luck didn't matter. He was exactly where he wanted to be.

"You bet your bushy beard we are."

14. EASTBORNE SOUR

Rhoren paced across the empty storefront. Nervous energy pulsed through his body while he waited for Kallum. He'd already swept and mopped the entire building in an attempt to keep himself busy.

Kallum was supposed to talk to Timofey today and finally reveal their plan to open a tavern. What if the owner of the Seaside Inn offered Kallum a better deal, or said something to give him second thoughts?

Rhoren wasn't sure he could make this work without Kallum.

When the doorknob finally clicked, Rhoren's chest felt like it was about to split in half.

Kallum entered carrying a basket filled with bottles. They clinked as he set the basket on the floor.

"Well?" Rhoren looked at him expectantly.

Kallum's face gave nothing away, then he sighed.

"That bad?" Rhoren grimaced.

Breaking the news to Timofey that Kallum was leaving had weighed on both of them for the past few days. In addition to his own worries about the business, it seemed likely that Rhoren wouldn't be welcome at the Seaside Inn after attempting to poach its bar manager. Even though it would have been easier to wait until the bar was near completion, they both agreed that it was better to be up front with Timofey so he could start his search for a replacement.

Judging by the look on Kallum's face, things hadn't gone well.

Kallum's mustache twitched, and his mouth curled at the edges. "I don't know why I was so worried. Timofey can be a hard-ass, but he's a good man. He wished us well and said he was sorry to see me go."

"Really?" Rhoren was shocked, but the tension released from his chest.

"Well, there were conditions, but I think he understands my desire to be a part of something from the ground up."

"A lifetime ban from the inn?"

"Not quite." Kallum laughed. "He gets to keep all of the recipes I created for the inn since I developed them while I was working there. It seemed like a fair trade for a peaceful parting of ways. He also said I can continue to work there as long as I would like. And no, you're not banned."

Rhoren sighed with relief. "Thank the gods. I wasn't looking forward to finding somewhere new to drink while we're getting this place up and running." He grinned. "That's great news, though! I just hope you have a few more recipes inside that head of yours."

"Remember the fit I was having because Timofey wouldn't let me spice up the menu?"

Rhoren nodded.

Kallum tapped the basket with his foot. "I figured now that the cat is out of the bag, we can start testing out some new recipes. Starting with the drink that stirred up such a fuss."

"What are we waiting for?" Rhoren rubbed his hands together in anticipation. "To the kitchen."

Kallum scoffed as he looked over Rhoren's dishware, which consisted of a single mug, a plate, a bowl, and one set of cutlery. "You want to open a bar and you can't even entertain a single guest?" He shook his head. "It's a good thing I brought my bartending kit."

Rhoren shrugged. "What can I say? I'm still a soldier at heart."

Kallum emptied his basket on the table and readied his ingredients for the first drink. "This one is a favorite of mine, and I was really hoping to get it on the menu at the inn. But Timofey's loss will be our gain. I call it the East-borne Sour. All of the ingredients from the rye wuiskey to the red wine used for the float are sourced from our fair city."

He started by pouring wuiskey into the shaker, followed by a squeeze of lemon and a splash of simple syrup.

"Normally, I would add some ice from the chiller to get this nice and cold. I guess that's something we'll have to decide on when the time comes. I'm sure they are pricey, but it wouldn't hurt to stop by the Tinkerer's Guild and see how much. Who knows what else those gnomish inventors might have come up with."

Rhoren nodded. "Sounds good to me."

After mixing the ingredients together, Kallum strained

the yellowish liquid into a glass. Then he popped the cork on a bottle of red wine, pouring it gently over the back of a spoon so that the wine floated at the top of the drink, creating a layer of red over the yellow.

"The key is to pour slowly to keep them from mixing. You'll want to use a dry red so that the tartness of the wine will really bring out the sweetness from the ingredients underneath. Give it a try."

Rhoren took the glass, holding it up to the light of the balcony and examining it from all angles. It was a visually appealing drink with the way the two colors played together.

The first sip was magnificent, overwhelmingly tart from the citrus but with a subtle sweetness layered underneath. There was also a hint of caramel from the wuiskey. He could imagine how much more refreshing it would be if it were chilled.

Rhoren took a bigger drink. "How could Timofey not want this on the menu?"

"He said it was too local. Apparently, a high-end inn needs more exotic items. I disagree. There are plenty of amazing spirits and wines across the realm, but there is nothing wrong with being proud of our city and the ingredients we produce. I think it's important to have a balance across the menu."

"I couldn't agree more."

The evening passed in a blur as Kallum showcased the skill that had landed him the job at the Seaside Inn to begin with. Every one of the drinks they tried was worthy of a place on the menu. The difficult part would be narrowing them down.

15. ALCHEMY

Over the next few weeks, the tavern began to slowly take shape. Kallum got a fair price from the builders, and despite the all-too-frequent complaints of Helena about the construction noise, a bar now ran along half of the right wall. There were plenty of shelves for bottles and glasses, as well as cabinets and nooks for storage. The tables, chairs, and other furniture would be arriving as the carpenters completed them.

Rhoren's days were filled with errands for the tavern, and there always seemed to be something new to add to the list. They still needed to see the weaver for tapestries and to visit the Tinkerer's Guild to check the price for a chiller. They'd narrowed down some of the recipes, but they would need to finalize the drink menu soon so that they could buy glassware and order the necessary alcohol.

And then there was the trouble with the rodent traps. It had taken every ounce of Rhoren's willpower to keep from using his blood sense when a trap was set off the previous night. Whatever rodents he was dealing with were crafty. He'd yet to catch one, and on more than one occasion, he'd come downstairs to find the traps empty of the cheese and not a creature in sight.

Rhoren refused to be outsmarted by vermin. If the bastards wanted to test his patience, he'd see how they felt once he laced the cheese with poison.

So instead of taking care of one of the many things on his to-do list, Rhoren found himself traveling south of the river to visit the alchemists.

The Warehouse District was the antithesis of the Trade District in almost every way. Trash lined the streets, and a layer of grime seemed to cover everything. Even the air felt heavy. North of the river, people were always on the move, and the streets flowed like the current with activity. This place was like a bog where people lurked, and a dozen eyes followed every move he made. The guards, who were a regular sight across the bridge, were almost non-existent here.

An acrid stench hit Rhoren like a wall as he passed through the gate to where the alchemists worked in isolation. High stone walls surrounded the alchemists' colony in an attempt to prevent their experiments from destroying entire city blocks. The mixture of chemicals made Rhoren's eyes water and the lingering smell of sulfur turned his stomach. He covered his nose with a kerchief and continued onward.

Each building was marked with a different symbol, none of which Rhoren recognized. Perhaps it was some secret language of the alchemists.

As he walked along the narrow streets, a huddled

figure grabbed him by the arm, scabbed fingers squeezing tight. "Beware the guardian of the night," they whispered. "She watches. Always watching."

Rhoren knelt, and the grip slackened. "Do you know where I can buy poison?"

"She watches. Always watching. Beneath the streets, she hunts for treats." The figure leaned forward, revealing a pox-marked face and decayed teeth before bursting into cackling laughter.

Rhoren shook his arm free and continued onward, careful to keep his arms close as he walked. The ramblings of a madman didn't disturb him. He'd seen it before in the Guard. The incoherent nonsense and ghastly expressions of those who'd come too close to death's door.

After wandering aimlessly through the streets, Rhoren found himself at a dead end. He turned around, approaching one of the cloaked figures that leaned against a marked building.

He hoped to have better luck this time. "Excuse me, do you know where I could buy some poison?"

The person looked up, and even though the majority of their face was concealed, a boil-covered nose escaped the cloak.

"What kind of poison?" a raspy voice asked as they extended a bandaged hand.

Rhoren placed a silver coin in their palm, not sure that he wanted to know how many different poisons they offered. "Something for rodents."

A wheezing cackle rattled within the cloak. "Rodents, yes. You'll find what you seek behind the door marked with the Igwaz."

Rhoren frowned. He assumed the Igwaz was one of the runes, but which one?

The hooded person held out their hand again, the coin Rhoren had given now gone.

With a sigh, he placed another coin in the bandaged palm.

The mysterious figure cleared their throat with a grating, phlegm-fueled sound. "Igwaz, the pitchfork." With that, they leaned back against the wall and sunk to the ground.

Rhoren continued his search before coming upon a building marked with a white rune resembling a pitchfork. He knocked, then stepped inside when no one answered.

The air inside the building was thick and heavy, with a faint hint of banana and peanuts. While more pleasant than the streets outside, Rhoren was almost certain the smell was the result of chemical reactions. He once again covered his nose and mouth with a kerchief out of caution.

Looking around, he immediately understood the dangers that the alchemists presented. The dimly lit building had no ventilation, and several cauldrons steamed and bubbled ominously. One, in particular, had an eerie green glow coming from within.

Luckily, there were no torches or candles burning. Instead, glowstones were mounted on the ceiling and walls, the enchanted rocks providing a hazy light over several of the workstations. Glowstones were hard to come by, but considering the experiments conducted within the walls of the colony, it was probably worth the expense. Jars of mysterious granulated crystals and liquids lined the shelves and tables, while taxidermied animals were scattered around the room, almost lifelike in their detail.

"How can I help you?" An alluring voice called from a dark corridor at the back. A moment later, a tall, auburn-haired woman stepped into the light. She wore black robes and a green-jeweled necklace that fell midway down her chest.

Her appearance took Rhoren by surprise. Her face was youthful, and she bore none of the physical deformities that he'd witnessed upon those on the streets.

"I was told to come here if I needed to buy poison. I have a bit of a rodent problem. The traps aren't working and they've learned to steal the bait without activating the trap at all."

The woman laughed. It was light and effervescent, a sharp contrast to the surroundings. "You've come to the right place."

Rhoren stepped forward. "I'll be honest. You're not exactly what I was expecting."

"Nor were you." She smirked. "What might the good people of Eastborne think if they knew an umbral elf was searching for poison among the alchemists?"

Rhoren stiffened, wondering if coming here had been a mistake.

"Don't worry, I jest." She came closer, and her eyes shimmered green with the reflection of the cauldron. "To most, the mystery of alchemy is a fear that rivals behemoths and krakens. In ages past, the alchemists were as revered as the mages."

"Is that so?" Rhoren had read stories of alchemists who achieved great things, creating wondrous potions, but also those who had been responsible for widespread destruction.

"It is. The catacombs that run beneath the northern half of the city were originally repurposed so that alchemists could move our creations out of sight of the public. After the explosion that leveled a temple and several surrounding blocks, we were relocated south of the river. But that was long before my time." She sighed, running her finger along the edge of the cauldron. "As they say, it only takes a few bad apples to ruin the bunch. For all the good we've done, it is the memory of destruction that lingers."

"I can understand that feeling." Blood mages were often regarded the same way in certain parts of the realm.

"Hmm." She raised an eyebrow. "You're here for poison, so tell me, what are we dealing with?"

"That's the thing, I'm not exactly sure. I haven't seen anything, but I keep hearing them at night, and every morning the cheese is gone."

She pressed a finger to her lips. "You can never underestimate a pest's will to survive. What part of the city are you in?"

Rhoren narrowed his brow. "Why does that matter?"

"Let me assure you, the vermin south of the river are a different breed." She frowned. "They require a more pernicious approach."

"I'm in the Trade District."

She opened her mouth as if to speak, but then she walked over to one of the shelves and grabbed a jar filled with a purple granulated substance. "Sprinkle this on your cheese. If there are rats or any other vermin, this will take care of them."

Rhoren took the jar, which was far heavier than it looked. "Any special instructions?"

"Don't eat it." She grinned. "And for the love of the gods, don't set it on fire."

16. THREADS OF FATE

"What do you mean the poison's not working?" Kallum asked as they entered the textile shop, Threads of Fate.

Rugs, tapestries, and woven baskets filled the spacious shop, each one meticulously crafted with images and colorful designs. At the back of the shop, there was the workspace where a mixture of half-finished tapestries and rugs awaited on looms. Spools of yarn in a myriad of colors lay scattered around while a man and woman worked the looms and a female halfling wove a basket in earnest.

The man turned from his project, waving at Rhoren and Kallum. "Be with you in a moment!"

Rhoren nodded before returning to the conversation. "I mean it's not working." He sighed, running his hand over a silk tapestry depicting the sun setting over a snow-capped mountain range. "I've tried everything. Stuffing the poison in cheese or pieces of bread. Sprinkling it on top. No matter what I do, it's like they know it's laced with poison. Every morning,

I come down and the food is sitting next to the traps."

"Uneaten?" Kallum frowned.

"Uneaten," Rhoren said with a scowl. "The bastards have the nerve to remove the bait from the trap and set it on the floor. It's like they're taunting me."

Kallum looked away to hide his grin. "And you still have no idea what's doing it?"

"It's not funny. I don't even know how they're getting inside." Rhoren rolled his eyes. "And no, I still haven't seen one, but at least the noise has stopped. So, I guess that's something."

Kallum faced Rhoren, placing a hand on each of his shoulders. "I'm glad that the vermin isn't waking you up at night, but we can't have rats, mice, or whatever else creeping through our tavern. It might be the norm south of the river, but not for what we're trying to do. Once we get a reputation for rats, no matter how smart they are, we might as well close up shop. It's humorous that they are taunting you, but we need to get this sorted."

Rhoren sighed again. The discomfort from the last time he'd used his abilities had nearly faded entirely. Waking up every day without aches and pains was a wonderful feeling. He'd vowed not to tap into his power for something as minor as this, but Kallum was right. They needed to solve this problem before they opened shop, and that day was getting closer.

He gripped Kallum on the upper arm. "I'll figure something out. For now, let's see about these tapestries."

Each tapestry was a work of art. While simpler variations could be found for cheaper in the lower levels of the city, these were more than just textiles. Each one took anywhere from weeks to months to create, and the price reflected as much. Tapestries like these were more than just decorations, they were a status symbol. They were talking points. But they wouldn't be anything if Rhoren didn't find a way to get rid of the damned pests.

"What can I help you gentlefolk with?" The man stepped through the gate separating the shop from the work area. He was tall and slender, with twig-like fingers perfect for working with yarn. A generous amount of stubble covered his face, and pieces of yarn clung to his tunic at odd angles.

"We were looking to buy a couple of tapestries." Kallum gestured toward the wall covered in detailed creations. "We're opening a tavern and we'd like to liven the place up."

"Most excellent!" The man bounced on his heels. "We do custom orders upon request, but the waitlist is quite extensive. We also have a selection of completed tapestries."

"You do exquisite work." Rhoren admired one depicting a kraken lurking underneath a ship. "We're looking to open soon, so I doubt we'll have time to wait for a custom piece."

"I do understand." He gestured around the shop. "Feel free to take a look around. There are notes pinned to each tapestry, but if you have any additional questions, don't hesitate to ask. My name is Hewelet."

Rhoren and Kallum walked the perimeter of the shop, admiring the pieces pinned to the walls. The first depicted the house crest of the royal family of Nelderland—a golden shield with a roaring bear positioned below a blue chevron. The family name, Torben, was on a banner above the shield, and the house motto "Steadfast and Gallant" on a banner below.

"I always found it odd that only four of the nine kingdoms are actual monarchies." Rhoren crossed his arms as he remembered his lessons from his first years in the Guard.

"Really?" Kallum raised his brows. "I know the halflings don't have a king, but I'm a bit embarrassed to say I don't know much about the others. I never paid much attention to the history lessons. The teacher was such a bore."

Rhoren laughed. "We were taught about all of the kingdoms, their leaders, and their governments in the Guard. It was important not only to know how to fight but to know what we were fighting for."

"I feel like we know so little of the Northern Guard this far south." Kallum placed a hand over his chest. "Would you care to enlighten this wretched soul on the politics of Aedrea?"

"How can I refuse a call like that?" Rhoren grinned. "I'm sure you're aware of this much at least, but only two of the three human kingdoms are monarchies. Nelderland, of course, and then there's Warminster, ruled by Queen Lilion. Gannett is governed by a republic."

"The stories I've heard about Queen Lilion." Kallum wiggled his brows. "They say she's a feisty one."

"I have no doubt. One doesn't rule over northerners without a bit of fire in their veins. Let's see. To the east of the human kingdoms, you have the dwarven lands. Rakroft is technically a dual monarchy. The Mountain King rules over the mountain dwarves of Mount Tor and the Hill King rules the lowland dwarves of Darm. Long ago, the two kingdoms were at war for nearly a hundred years. It's said that one of their battles awakened a sleeping dragon, and that is the reason it burned Hells' Crag to ruins. Either way, the dragon attack ended the war and the two kings reasoned that they were stronger together."

Kallum nodded along. "I do remember that story. An entire city turned to rubble." Kallum held up four fingers. "If those are the four kingdoms, then what are the others?"

"The gnomes have a council, with a chancellor as the head of state. The halflings have a commonwealth, and the elder elves have a triarchy ruled by three mages."

"And what about your people?"

The history of the umbral elves was a story in itself. They were outcasts more than anything, and with the frozen north above them and the wilds to the east, survival often took priority over politics.

"We have a Bulwark. They're responsible for the protection of Cascus, though a council offers advice."

"I feel smarter already." Kallum tapped his temple before pointing to a tapestry featuring a mage facing a terrifying red dragon. Energy extended from the mage's staff, forking in several directions. "I can't imagine what it would be like to have the kind of power that even dragons fear."

Rhoren read the note pinned to the tapestry. *Raglan the Magnificent battles a red dragon.* He knew the story well. After Hells' Crag was left in ruins, the red dragon turned its eyes to the west. Raglan singlehandedly pushed the dragon back, giving it such grievous wounds that it retreated to the surrounding mountains. The mage died from the encounter. Not from the battle itself but from the mana drain on his body.

He clenched his fingers, searching for the almost non-existent tingle that had once been a daily occurrence. When a mage depleted their mana reserves, magic ravaged their bodies no differently than blood magic.

Magic always had a cost. Power must come from somewhere, and with mages, it came from mana. For blood mages, that power came from within.

Rhoren stared at the tapestry, at the moment frozen in time. "That kind of power only comes around once in a generation. It usually takes an entire party of mages to even gain the attention of a red dragon. Mages like Raglan become legend. There's no telling how many lives he saved with his actions."

"Tonight, we can toast to Raglan." Kallum moved to the next tapestry with a scene depicting a field of golden sunflowers. A griffin flew over the flowers, wings spread wide.

They made their way around the shop, searching for the perfect fit for their tavern.

"Look, this one has the crest of the Northern Guard!" Kallum grabbed Rhoren by the arm, pulling him over to his location and clapping his hands together. "We have to get this one for the tavern."

The tapestry had the sigil of the Northern Guard, a shield emblazoned with three mountain peaks, in the lower half of the piece, while the top half showcased a beautiful and snowy mountain range. The image brought back memories of his adventures beyond the outpost. It would be a nice addition to the tavern.

"You sure?" Rhoren asked.

"Of course. You've spent your life serving the realm. It's a part of you." He tapped Rhoren's chest, where the Guard's sigil had been embroidered on his old robes. "I remember the first time you came into the Seaside Inn, weary from travel and still wearing your uniform. Just because you're starting the next chapter of your life doesn't mean you have to forget what shaped you." He waved to Hewelet. "We'll take this one."

"A fan of the Northern Guard?" Hewelet came over and unpinned the tapestry.

"You could say that." Kallum winked at Rhoren. "This one was an officer."

Hewelet's eyes widened in surprise. "Well, in that case. I'll give it to you at a discount. For your service."

"You don't have to do that." Rhoren waved his hand as if to banish the idea.

"And you didn't have to defend the realm." Hewelet folded the tapestry and set it aside. "Working with tapestries is a lot like being a scholar. We read and learn about the subjects that we depict. I am well-aware of the role the Guard plays for the health of the realm, even if most this far south are not."

Rhoren nodded graciously. There was no point in contradicting the man. Telling him that blood mages had no choice in their enrollment in the Guard would mean explaining to Kallum that he was more than just a soldier. He still wasn't ready for that conversation.

They still needed to pick a second tapestry to frame the fireplace, and Rhoren told Kallum that the final choice would be his. They continued their search, reading about the crests of famous families and historical moments rendered in amazing detail through yarn.

"This one is kind of spooky." Kallum stopped in front of a tapestry with a much darker color scheme than the others.

It showed a graveyard filled with tombstones beneath a full moon. A black fox with three glowing blue tails walked among the graves. The piece was titled *Spirit Fox. Guardians of the night. Watchers of the dead.*

Rhoren froze, remembering the ramblings of the lurker in the alchemist colony. *"Beware the guardian of the night,"* the voice had whispered. *"She watches. Always watching."*

"What?" Kallum gave him a concerned look.

"It's nothing." Rhoren frowned. "Well, likely nothing. When I went to buy poison, there was this man. He kept rambling about the guardian of the night. None of it made any sense."

"Let's get to the bottom of it then." Kallum waved toward the back. "Excuse me, Hewelet, could you tell us a little more about this piece?"

Hewelet paused his work and came over. "Ah, the spirit fox, a Nelderland legend. They are said to guard over the dead, and that their glowing tails keep evil spirits at bay. Some say they've seen the spirit fox appear in visions while in the midst of great tragedy, a watchful protector."

"Are they real?" asked Rhoren.

"Are behemoths real? What about the fae that lurk within the Vaglir Forest or the banshees of the wilds?" Hewelet shrugged. "I may not have seen them myself, but I do not doubt their existence. I've found that all legends have some basis in truth."

Rhoren knew firsthand the existence of behemoths.

He'd seen ice dragons soaring high above the mountain peaks and had encountered direwolves and griffins. If all those things existed, why not krakens and spirit foxes?

In the end, Kallum chose a tapestry that spoke to him. It pictured a cloaked rider traveling down an empty road. Fall trees lined both sides of the path, their leaves a mixture of red, gold, and orange with a cloudless blue sky overhead.

Hewelet folded the tapestry and placed it on top of the other in a wooden crate.

Kallum rested his hand on the piece of art. "It seemed fitting. We don't know where he's coming from or where he's going, only what we see in this brief instance. That's how bartending is most of the time, a snippet of someone's life as they come and go."

"I like that." Rhoren paid for the tapestries, and they were on their way.

The tapestries were thick and made from quality wool. Even with Rhoren and Kallum each taking a side of the crate, it was heavier than either would like to carry through the city. So, they flagged down a cart to take them back to the Trade District.

"Jesper!" Rhoren grinned as the former farmhand came to a stop. "I was wondering when I would see you again."

Jesper wiped a sweaty strand of hair from his brow. "Good to see you! I haven't had many trips up your way of late. To the Seaside Inn?"

"Not this time. Do you remember the shop you showed me?"

Jesper's eyes went wide. "You didn't?"

"I did. I'll give you the tour once we arrive."

The young man grunted as he lifted the crate into the back of the cart, his muscles flexing from the strain. "What are you hiding underneath these blankets?"

"Not blankets. Tapestries." Rhoren tapped the side of the crate. "My business partner and I are opening a tavern and we needed something to liven the place up."

"That would be me." Kallum extended a hand. "I'm Kallum. Nice to meet you."

Jesper took Kallum's hand, narrowing his eyes as recognition dawned on him. "Aren't you the bartender from the inn?"

"Not for much longer."

"Opening a tavern in a cursed building. You two are crazier than you look." Jesper shook his head as he took the cart in both hands and started the trek up the city.

While they traveled, Rhoren explained the situation with the rodent traps and the poison. Jesper laughed so hard that he had to stop the cart at one point.

"What's so funny?" asked Rhoren.

"You city folk with your traps and your poisons." He laughed again. "If you want to keep the pests away from your livelihood, what you need is a cat."

Rhoren exchanged a glance with Kallum. Why hadn't he thought of that before? Every stable in the Guard had a barn cat to keep the rats out of the feed. A cat seemed like a great solution to the problem.

After paying Jesper for the ride, Rhoren jingled a few more silver coins in his palm. "What are the chances you can find me a cat?"

17. BLOOD OF THE PHOENIX

"Dammit, Jinx! Get down." Rhoren scolded the giant fluff of a beast that sat on the glimmering bar top.

The cat sat there, unfazed, licking his giant paw. Jesper had shown up several days prior with the massive beast cradled against his broad shoulders. Jinx was quite handsome with luxurious golden-brown fur and striking green eyes. Dark tufts of hair outlined the tips of his ears, along with a regal mane and equally imposing paws.

Rhoren wondered where Jesper had found such a beautifully menacing animal, but he refused to reveal any of the details regarding the cat's origin, only saying that it wasn't stolen. As long as no one showed up looking for a missing pet, Rhoren was fine letting the mystery linger.

Considering the disdain most people had for this building in the first place, Jinx felt like the perfect name for something meant to put a stop to the noises that had evicted the previous tenants.

Rhoren narrowed his eyes at Jinx as the cat continued to lick his dangerous paws. "How many times do I have to tell you? You have free run of the place, just. Not. On. The. Bar!" He swiped at Jinx with a polishing towel.

Taking offense, Jinx swatted back, gathering the rag in his claws and leaping to the floor with a soft patter. He rolled around, attacking the towel with fervor.

"We're going to have to put a stop to that." Rhoren huffed.

"Give it time." Kallum looked away to conceal his laughter. "At least the noises have stopped, right?"

Rhoren crossed the bar and knelt, tugging at the towel as Jinx curled around it, kicking at the fabric opponent with his back legs. As annoying as the little beast was, Rhoren had grown attached to him rather quickly.

"There is that." He petted Jinx on the head, and the cat forgot about his new enemy, nuzzling against Rhoren's leg with a purr. "I just wish he wasn't so stubborn."

"I take it you've never spent time around a cat. They're all assholes." Kallum finished muddling a lime in the bottom of the glass and added a pour of rhum. "Come tell me what you think of this one?"

Rhoren gave Jinx a scratch behind the ear before taking a seat at the bar. The furniture had all been delivered, and now stools lined the bar. A half-dozen tables took up most of the floor space aside from the leather sofa and two oversized chairs in front of the fireplace. With the tapestries hung to each side, the space was finally coming together. Barring any setbacks, they would be ready to open within the month.

"What's this one called again?" Rhoren asked as he raised the glass, observing the muddled lime that gave it a nice green color.

"The Pleasant Peasant. It's a coastal staple and pretty

quick to make. It's a good one to recommend when the bar is full and you need to get the drinks out fast."

Rhoren gulped. The idea of a full bar both excited and terrified him. As much as the prospect of bringing his father's drinks to life thrilled him, he was completely out of his element when it came to making drinks. The other night, he'd awoken in a cold sweat after dreaming of a packed bar. Rowdy customers shouted at him for drinks, and no matter how fast he worked, the orders never stopped coming. He had called to Kallum for help, but his business partner was nowhere to be found.

He took a sniff of the cocktail, and the citrus aroma cleared his mind. The first sip was a surprise, pleasantly sweet despite the abundance of lime. The drink was smooth and refreshing, and with a little ice, it would be the perfect offering for a warm summer day.

"This is good." He took another drink. "Delicious."

"You ready to give it a shot?" Kallum smirked.

Rhoren set the glass down. Even though they'd been practicing, he still didn't feel very comfortable behind the bar. In all his years in the Guard, he'd never had a night-mare about the monsters he'd faced, yet the thought of bartending gave him sweaty palms. Why had he thought opening a tavern was a good idea?

When he compared himself to Kallum, he felt like a newborn foal standing next to a stallion. Kallum's every movement was graceful. Even though the bar was new to them both, it was as if the space was an extension of the man. His pours were smooth, and he worked with the finesse of someone who had spent their entire life crafting drinks.

And then there was Rhoren. He fumbled his movements and took way too long deciding which ingredients the drinks required, even when Kallum would list them out for him. His pours were sloppy and often spilled down the outside of the glassware.

"Hey, it gets easier with practice." Kallum walked around the bar and took a seat next to Rhoren. "I can see the panic in your eyes every time you pick up the bottle. Let me tell you, the first time I ever got behind the bar, I spilled a drink on the customer as I was handing them the glass. It went everywhere. I was mortified, but you know what? At the end of the day, we're making drinks. No one is going to die because you spilled some rhum or forgot an ingredient. If someone has a problem, give them a double pour and that usually shuts them up."

Rhoren smiled. "I'm glad you're around to show me the ropes."

"Yeah, yeah. Now, quit stalling and make me a drink."

Rhoren recalled the recipe for The Pleasant Peasant. It was one of the simpler drinks to make, only requiring three ingredients—limes, sugar, and white rhum.

First, he sliced the lime into eighths and dropped them in the glass, along with two cubes of sugar. As he muddled the lime, the juice exploded inside the glass, helping to break down the sugar cubes. Once there was a syrupy puddle of lime juice, he added the rhum.

Kallum grinned from across the bar.

"What? Did I miss something?" Rhoren frowned as he replayed the steps in his mind.

"Not at all." Kallum placed the drink he'd made next to Rhoren's. "Look, you can't even tell a difference. Well done!"

Rhoren picked up the drinks, examining them both.

He smiled as he handed one to Kallum. "Cheers." Their glasses clinked, and Jinx leapt onto the bar and plopped down. "Cheers to you, too, big fella."

As they enjoyed the drinks, Kallum grabbed Rhoren's father's journal from the end of the bar. "I've been poring through the recipes in here, and there are so many good options." He flipped through the pages. "It's been hard to choose, but I think this one would be a perfect fit."

He turned the journal to face Rhoren, tapping the top of the page titled Blood of the Phoenix.

Blood of the Phoenix

Ingredients:

2 oz Mezcalium
.25 cup fresh blood orange juice
1 tbsp fresh lime juice
.25 cup fresh grapefruit juice
3 oz blood orange soda
blood orange for garnish

There were sketches of fruit and a spiked plant to one side of the page. Beneath the recipe, there were the customary notes on the taste and appearance.

Taste: *Well-balanced, citrusy, and slightly bitter from the grapefruit juice. Sweet and slightly tart.*

Appearance: *Pinkish-red, though much depends on the*

coloring of the blood oranges. The drink can be garnished with a blood orange slice or wheel. For added flavor, coat the rim in a chili-lime seasoning.

Below the tasting notes, Rhoren's father had scribbled even more detailed notes on the region and the drink's history.

My travels along the coast of Gannet have been some of the fondest I can remember. The people here are unlike any other throughout the realm. Time seems to move slower here. There's no hurry, and the customary afternoon naps would make the halflings proud. I've been introduced to food and drink that I will savor for all my days.

The southern coast of Gannet may be the only location in the realm capable of sustaining the ingredients for the Blood of the Phoenix. It is a shame, because the world over deserves to taste its magnificence. The locals use the leaves of a local plant to make the mezcalium. Due to the way the plant is roasted during the process, it gives the alcohol a smokey taste that's incomparable.

Peppers and citrus are a staple of Gannet cuisine, and both have found their way into the local drinks as well. For me, I have found a deep fondness for the blood orange. It is smaller than a typical orange, but sweeter, and with flesh the deep red of freshly-drawn blood. I believe it has the ability to be the core component for some truly visually stunning cocktails.

Perhaps one of my greatest discoveries was the existence of soda water. There is a natural spring near Crowhold that produces water that fizzes and sparkles. They say the natural minerals in the spring are responsible for this phenomenon. Regardless, some of the local bartenders have found ways to utilize it in their drinks. By mixing soda water with fresh juice, and a small amount of simple sugar, they have created a refreshing beverage that livens up any gathering, even more so when alcohol is added to the mix. The soda water can be bottled, and though the fizziness fades over time once opened, it can be preserved for weeks or months as long as it remains sealed.

Rhoren traced his father's words as he read them. "I've always wondered about this one. There's enthusiasm in most of his notes, but nothing compares to how he talked of his time in Gannett."

"The way your father described it, I was tempted to leave Eastborne and move there myself." Kallum grinned. "I had to call in some favors, but I think I can get us a steady supply of soda water from Crowhold."

Rhoren's eyes filled with excitement. "That's amazing." He lifted his drink again, tilting it toward Kallum. "You're amazing."

Kallum's cheeks flushed. "I've made a lot of connections during my years at the Seaside Inn. What better time to use them than right now?"

Jinx interrupted the conversation by swatting an errant lime off the bar. The cat looked at Rhoren before he leapt to the floor, speeding across the room and up the stairs like a demon fresh out of hell.

"Gods help us." Rhoren frowned as he picked up the lime.

Kallum laughed. "This is going to be so much fun."

18. PROPOSITIONS

The days continued to fly by, and while Kallum set out to purchase glassware for the bar, Rhoren headed toward the docks. Talking to the food cart vendors was one of the final tasks, and he hoped that they would see the benefit that a partnership could have for both of their businesses.

As Rhoren entered the port of Eastborne, the sun shone bright and a warm breeze tousled his hair. Seagulls cawed, and the sounds of dockworkers unloading cargo filled the air.

A group of elder elves exited a ship that sported emerald-green sails. The hull of the ship was pearlescent white and gleamed against the calm surface of the bay. The elves walked with their heads held high, blonde hair and ivory skin practically glowing in the sun. Such a stark contrast from his own. It was uncommon for elder elves to travel far from their homeland, and he couldn't help but wonder what brought them this far to the west.

Several guards greeted the elves as they exited the ship, escorting them to a covered wagon topped with the banner of Eastborne. The guard's attire was the same as those that stood sentry outside of the gates to the Council District.

Everywhere Rhoren turned, people were coming and going. Compared to the other districts of Eastborne, the docks were a melting pot of different races, stations, and classes. Laborers, traders, travelers, and dignitaries walked amongst one another as they attended their business.

People gathered around what appeared to be a famous mage as she boarded a ship. She waved at the crowd, performing a display of fire magic before disappearing onto the deck.

Rhoren had often wondered what it would be like to be celebrated for his powers instead of feared. Sure, he was respected in the north, but it was a respect born of fear for the devastation he could cause, not from wonder or amazement. Blood didn't sparkle or ignite. It wasn't wondrous to behold.

He returned to the task at hand, finding a steady supply of food for the tavern. There were vendors scattered around the docks, but Rhoren wanted to start with one in particular. He passed a cart with an oven mounted on the back selling freshly-baked pretzels. There was another selling meat pies. The smell was so savory and enticing that he could imagine it luring customers to the tavern from blocks away. He made a mental note to return to those but kept his eye out for a portly man selling oysters.

He found Dingo stationed near a passenger ship with his cart of oysters and bread, luring people over with his boisterous voice as they disembarked. The man's eyes went wide when he noticed Rhoren approaching. His large mustache twitched, but since it covered his lips, Rhoren couldn't read much into the man's expression.

Rhoren smiled as he tried to break the ice. "How's business?"

He looked over the contents of the cart. There were fresh oysters, sliced lemons, and a basket with several loaves of bread. A rack with bottles of vinegar hung to the side of the cart, where a woman doused vinegar on a pair of oysters before taking off into the city.

Dingo moved the oysters around in a more appealing fashion. "It comes and goes with the tides. Haven't seen you around these parts lately." He raised a brow. "Come to check in on me?"

"I've been busy. That's partly why I'm here." He picked up a few oysters. "I also wanted to see if you'd seen James and Cindy around."

Rhoren had told the two children to come by the Seaside Inn if they ever needed anything, but so far, they hadn't visited. And with all the work at the bar, he hadn't been down to the docks since their first meeting.

Dingo frowned, looking out to sea. "They came around often after the incident. They're good kids, and I feel bad for how I handled the situation to begin with. There was a time when I was running around the docks no differently. Some things never change, I suppose." He sold a half-loaf of bread and three oysters to a grungy-looking man with an unkempt beard but continued talking. "At first, they came around every couple of days. I'd give them some bread and an apple if I had any. They would take the food and leave. Eventually, they started hanging around and I got to know them a little. The boy is smart, and the girl, she's funny. I used to know their old man in my younger days. Tomas. He's good people. It's been a few weeks since I've last seen them, though."

"You think everything is okay?" Rhoren asked.

"You know how it goes." Dingo nodded at a man passing by. "Their father is a sailor. He comes and goes. If I had to guess, I would say they'll be back around in time."

"Well, this is if they come back around." Rhoren pulled a gold coin from his purse. "You wouldn't happen to know where they live, do you?"

Dingo frowned as he slipped the coin into his apron pocket. "I can't say for sure. I know they live down by the stables. If you head that way, you might find someone who knows them."

Rhoren started that way before realizing he hadn't mentioned the reason he'd come down to the docks to begin with.

He turned around, grinning. "Before I go, I have a business proposition for you."

Dingo leaned forward, his mustache twitching on one side in what Rhoren assumed was a smile. "This will be interesting."

Rhoren filled the oyster vendor in on his plans for the bar and a potential partnership with a different food cart for each night of the week. "During the day, you move your cart from one location to another, always having to track down people to buy your food, but we'll have clientele who are hungry and ready to spend money. All you have to do is show up and bring your cart."

Dingo stroked his mustache. "It's not a half-bad plan. And you want a different cart each night of the week?"

Rhoren nodded. "Exactly, like a rotating menu. It's a win-win proposition for all those involved."

He tapped his chin contemplatively. "I'll need to talk it over with my wife, but I like the idea of it."

"Think it over and get back to me. I've got a few more vendors to talk to and then some kids to wrangle."

Rhoren faced the sprawling city before him, wondering if that might be easier said than done.

To put it simply, the Lower District south of the river reeked. The stench of manure, urine, and animal hides pervaded everything. Not even the coastal breeze could cleanse the area of the fetor. With the stables, tannery, and butcher all situated within spitting distance of one another, Rhoren wondered how anyone was capable of breathing at all. He'd seen the process used to strip the hair from animal hides in the Guard, and he scrunched his nose just thinking about it.

A section of housing ran between the Lower District and the Warehouse District. This was supposedly where James and Cindy lived. Dingo said a lot of the dock-workers and sailors had settled in the area, and that they looked out for their own. The smell wasn't as bad, but it could hardly be called pleasant.

Rhoren was surprised when he came upon another umbral elf walking the streets. The dark-skinned elf wore a faded tan tunic, a blue vest with several buttons missing, and flowing brown trousers. A black sash and belt wrapped around his waist with a cutlass hanging to one side. He carried a satchel over one shoulder but set it on the ground when he saw Rhoren, his red eyes full of intrigue. The two stood like statues, staring at each other in disbelief for a moment.

"Sorry." Rhoren cleared his throat. "You're the first one of us I've seen since coming here."

The elf chuckled. "There aren't many of us here." He looked Rhoren up and down. "You seem to be doing well for yourself. Where are you from?"

Rhoren was suddenly aware of how fine his clothing was compared to those around him. They might be simple by the standards north of the river, but they were still well made. "I'm from Hollowton originally, but I served in the Guard. How'd you find your way this far south?"

"You're a better elf than me to risk life and limb for the realm." He grinned, and a gold tooth sparkled in the sun. "I grew up in Sanguine. Left the first chance I could on a trade wagon heading south. I never liked the cold that much to begin with."

Rhoren smiled at the elf's honesty. "Sailor?"

"Of a sort." His lip curled in a wicked smile.

Rhoren nodded his understanding. "You familiar with these parts? I'm trying to find a couple of kids that live around here."

He gave Rhoren a questioning look.

"Just to make sure they're okay," Rhoren added.

"Aren't you a noble spirit? I don't know much of the comings and goings around here, but if you go see Ol' Bessy, she might can help. That woman has a nose for gossip if anyone does." He pointed over his shoulder. "She's three streets up that way. You can't miss her."

"Thanks, uh…"

"Barryth." He picked up his bag and tossed it over his shoulder. "Good luck with your search."

True to Barryth's words, Ol' Bessy wasn't hard to find. She leaned out from a second-floor balcony, long gray hair tossed over the side like a curtain, talking to everyone who walked past, whether they responded or not. Her arms were like twigs caught in a tempest, moving animatedly with her every word. Some waved, others stopped for a moment to chat, but the elderly woman leaned over the railing so far that Rhoren was worried she might topple into the street.

"You there!" She pointed at Rhoren. "Come tell Ol' Bessy what brings you around here. Oh no, don't be shy. I know someone searching for answers when I see them. Ol' Bessy doesn't miss a thing, let me tell you. No, sir, if it's happening in these streets, you best believe I know about it."

"Come on, Grandma, leave the poor man alone." A young woman stepped onto the balcony, her vibrant red hair hanging to her waist. She gave Rhoren an apologetic look.

"That's no man." Ol' Bessy frowned at her grand-daughter. "I may be old, but I've still got the eyes of a hawk. That's an elf, and he's searching for something."

"Someone, actually." Rhoren raised his voice so she could hear him. "Or someones, I guess. I was told you might be able to help with that."

"See? I told you." Ol' Bessy waved her granddaughter away before returning her attention to Rhoren. "Come and tell Ol' Bessy who it is you're searching for."

As awkward as he felt having a conversation with a loud old woman in front of everyone on the street,

Rhoren stepped closer. This was the only lead he had for the children's whereabouts, and there was still much to do for the bar.

He couldn't explain why he felt so compelled to check on their well-being, but he was determined to see it through.

Rhoren cleared his throat. "There are a pair of siblings, James and Cindy. I ran into them down by the pier a few weeks back. I haven't seen them around and wanted to see how they were."

"Ah, yes." Her face dawned with recognition. "The Crookshank kids. The boy can be a bit mischievous, but the girl is sweet as pie—for now, at least. When your father is a sailor, it leaves too much time for a young girl to get into trouble. Ol' Bessy has seen it more times than you can count."

The old woman was a gossip, that was for sure, and she clearly loved to hear herself talk. Rhoren interrupted her as she went on a diatribe about the women she'd seen lose their innocence, and the sailors who went out to sea and never returned.

"Sorry, but do you happen to know where I might find them? I'm in a bit of a hurry today."

"Of course you are. Everyone is always in a hurry these days. Not Ol' Bessy, though. Slow it down, I say. Better to keep the devils at bay." She scoffed. "Tomas lives down the way, two streets over. His door is marked with the sailor's crest. His ship came in a fortnight ago."

Rhoren said his thanks and left before she had time to go on another rant.

"Hey, come back here!" she shouted after him as he turned the corner.

Finding the house was easier said than done, as many of the doors were marked with the sailor's crest— two triangles, one on top of the other, with a vertical line going through both. A rudimentary depiction of open sails on a mast. Supposedly, the mark kept their possessions safe while they were out to sea. Rhoren knew firsthand how members of the Guard looked out for one another, and he assumed this was the same.

After asking around, he found out which house belonged to the Crookshanks. Like most of the housing in the area, it was in disrepair. A life on the seas didn't leave much time for home maintenance. There were visible cracks in the wood, and one of the shutters was barely covering the window. Given that Eastborne was in a temperate climate, it probably didn't matter too much.

Rhoren knocked, but there was no one home. He was about to head back when he heard the laughter of a young girl from down the street.

"Look!" she shouted with glee. "It's the elf I told you about."

Rhoren turned to see the two children to each side of a tall man. Cindy waved, and James seemed less haggard than he had at the pier, like a weight had been lifted from his shoulders. Cindy held the man's hand, skipping along the street.

The man, who Rhoren assumed was Tomas, had the same blonde hair as both children. His skin was tan and freckled from the sun, and even though he was thin, there was a strength about him from years of hard labor.

"Well, I'll be…" His voice trailed off.

"I told you, Daddy." Cindy grinned. "He's a nice elf."

Their father stammered for a moment before

regaining his composure. "Apologies. When she told me she had lunch with an elf down by the pier, it seemed a bit far-fetched." He ruffled Cindy's hair. "I certainly learned my lesson, little lady."

"No worries." Rhoren chuckled, extending his hand. "I'm Rhoren. They told me you were a sailor. No one had seen them around for a few weeks so I thought I would drop by and make sure everything was okay."

"That's awfully kind of you. I'm Tomas. My ship got in a couple of weeks ago." He squeezed James on the shoulder. "Thought it was time to give the man of the house a break. He does a good job of keeping everything in order while I'm gone."

James stood a little straighter, puffing his chest out at the compliment.

"That he does." Rhoren winked at James. "I'll leave you be then. How long before you set sail again?"

Tomas shrugged. "Maybe a week or two. It's hard to say. We set out once we have enough cargo to move."

"Well, I'm in the process of opening a tavern in the Trade District. If you're still around, you should stop by for the grand opening. We'll have food for the kids."

"We'll see." Tomas's gaze drifted toward the street. "No promises, but we'll see."

Rhoren's cheeks grew hot. He'd meant the offer free of charge, but now an awkwardness lingered in the air. He wracked his brain for a way to invite them without making it seem like a handout.

He slid his boots across the street nervously. "I was going to pitch the idea once you'd seen the place, but we're going to need a barback to clean the glassware and wipe the tables once business picks up. You think that's something James would be interested in?"

James's eyes went wide, but he waited for his father to speak.

Tomas looked at his son and smiled. "He is almost that age, isn't he? What do you think, son?"

"A real job?" James's grin stretched from ear to ear. "When can I start?"

Rhoren and Tomas both laughed.

19. RUNECRAFTING

Rhoren had always found gnomes to be quite intriguing. Not for their jewel-toned hair or short stature, but for their industrious and innovative nature. As a race, they were pushing Aedrea toward the next age at a prodigious rate. While their inventions had always been worthy of being called a spectacle, they had recently begun to embark down more practical avenues, using the art of runecrafting to change the very way of life for their people.

Many mages had a disdain toward this new way of thinking, taking offense to a contraption that could mimic the powers of those empowered by the gods.

Rhoren had never felt that way. His powers hardly ever felt blessed. If the gnomes could invent weapons capable of fighting off behemoths, he would celebrate their achievement. Alas, the gnomish council had passed laws to stop the runecrafting of weapons. Enchanted weapons still existed in the world, and they were prized by adventurers, but most were from ages past, and new weapons were crafted in secret.

His father had traveled to Aethervale, the twin islands to the west of the continent, and learned to make several cocktails while there. The gnomish lands were also home to some of the greatest scholars, inventors, and runecrafters throughout the realm, and their university was regarded by most as the preeminent educational institution. According to Charence, the gnomes had nurtured a society built on curiosity by pressing the boundaries of magic and technology. Runetech, they called it. Which was part of the reason Rhoren and Kallum found themselves inside the Aethervale Guild of Tinkerers, Runecrafters, and Magical Engineers.

The windowless building was located within the Guild District. Brilliant white marble gave the building an air of mystery, drawing the eye but offering little insight as to what awaited inside.

Their teal-haired guide led them down a hallway toward the guild showroom. Her shimmering hair draped over her shoulders, and though she barely came up to either of their waists, she had an authority about her.

A soot-covered gnome slammed a door as he stepped into the hallway. His hair stood on end, frizzled. When he removed his goggles, the absence of soot left him looking like a masked raccoon.

"One of these days." He sighed. "One of these days."

"Are you familiar with runecrafting?" Their guide asked as they passed by, her voice high-pitched and nasally.

"Somewhat," answered Rhoren. He'd studied runes during his youth but quickly found that he didn't have the runecrafter's touch. Runecrafting took a delicate hand and an amazing amount of skill to harness the power of the elements within the ancient symbols.

"Not really," Kallum said sheepishly.

"Do not worry." She smiled, turning to face them. "Many call runes the Language of the Gods and believe them to have been passed down from the gods themselves. Anyone is capable of carving or writing runes, so long as they have the skill, but there are only a select few capable of charging runes and calling forth their power. We call them runecrafters. They are similar to mages in a way, acting as a conduit between item and mana. Mana fills the rune, and depending on the inscriptions and capacity of the item, it acts accordingly."

She led them into the showroom, stopping at a table topped with polished rocks in a variety of colors. "Take these glowstones, for example. They are etched with the rune for light. That alone does nothing, but once it is charged, the power from the rune ignites the stone."

"How are they charged?" asked Kallum.

"The runecrafter must sit with the item, channeling mana until a sufficient charge is set. Depending on the power of the item, this can take minutes, hours, or days."

"Fascinating." Kallum leaned in closer, inspecting the multi-colored light of the glowstones. "Are there ways to speed up the process?"

"There are." She winked. "Certain locations in Aedrea seem to be richer in mana than others, Aethervale being one of them. It also helps to be near the element you are trying to imbue into the object. For a glowstone, light. For a heater, fire. For a chiller..."

"Ice or cold," Kallum answered excitedly.

"Exactly." She went from one glowstone to the other, showing how each one had a different color and brightness.

"May I?" Rhoren gestured to one of the items.

She nodded, and he picked it up. He'd seen them before in the Guard, used on occasions when carrying a torch was dangerous or impractical. Unlike a torch, the glowstone produced no heat, just a gentle light. The only problem was it took someone capable of working with runic magic to deactivate the light. The charge could last for years, but the glowstone had to be concealed under a thick cloth when it wasn't needed.

"Is there a limit to how much you can charge it? For instance, could it be charged to cast a beam of light instead of a glow?"

She took the stone back from him. "Testing the limits of runecrafting is a dangerous road. It is a delicate balance to determine how much mana an object may hold. Too little, and the charge fades too quickly. Too much, and, well, you saw our friend back there. If you're unlucky, you might lose a finger, a hand, or worse." She gave him a knowing look.

Setting the glowstone back on the table, she led them to a contraption called a heater. The device featured an enchanted stone encased in a metal box. The box was warm and hot air escaped through the vents in the top.

"As you can imagine, a portable heat source is convenient, but also dangerous. One can't simply douse a heater with water to cool it off. The heat will continue until the charge fades, regardless of the season. One of the major disadvantages of Runetech is that only runecrafters are capable of activating and deactivating runes. So far, our experiments into activation switches have not been fruitful."

After showing them several other devices and mechanisms powered by runes, she led them to the chillers.

"Aside from the glowstones, these have been one of our greater achievements. They can be crafted in different sizes and temperatures, from a cold that prolongs the storage of ready-to-eat food to frigid temperatures capable of preventing ice from melting. We even have a design with a partition to do both."

Kallum rubbed his hands together. "Now, we're talking!"

The chiller was a simple device in its design, a metal cube or rectangle with a hinged door and a handle to open it. Runes glowed on the outside of the box, and when opened, a frigid fog poured out.

"How much are we looking at?" Kallum asked as he open several chillers, measuring them with a piece of rope he'd cut to match the height of the bar.

"That depends." The guide gestured between two different models. "Your basic version will run about five thousand gold. The partitioned models go up to around ten thousand."

Rhoren gulped. That was a lot of coin. Over the past few months, the expenses had continued to mount. With the cost of the building, the construction, and all of the alcohol and glassware, purchasing a chiller would likely tap his savings dry. He'd still have his pension from retirement, but after this, the bar would be forced to survive on its own, for better or for worse.

Kallum rested a hand on his shoulder and leaned in. "We don't have to get this, you know. It's a luxury. All of our drinks will stand on their own without it, and we can purchase ice by the day from somewhere else."

"No." Rhoren shook his head. "If we're going to do this, we're going to do it right." He met Kallum's gaze, and bright blue eyes stared at him intently. "I believe in you. I believe in us. We can make this work."

Kallum's firm squeeze on his shoulder was all the reassurance he needed.

He returned his attention to the guide. "Show us what you've got."

One by one, they went through the various models, discussing the pros and cons of each. The larger chillers were easy to dismiss, as well as those with partitions. Since they weren't storing food, they had no need for anything less than freezing temperatures.

In the end, they decided on a chiller that would fit perfectly behind the bar. It had a shelf in the middle and could fit two large blocks of ice. All they had to do was fill the metal tub with water, and the water would freeze overnight.

Rhoren's hand hovered above the contract, quill in hand. He looked to Kallum for reassurance, and when the man nodded, he signed his name to the parchment. The coin was spent. Hopefully, well-spent.

20. CURSED COCKTAILS

The cart driver waited patiently while Rhoren and Kallum unloaded crates of alcohol for the bar. Apparently, delivery service ended at the doorstep. Straw and sawdust lined the crates, protecting the bottles on their long journeys. Some had come from as far as Aethervale to the west and Greenbriar Marsh to the east.

"Looks like you fellas are almost ready." Titus's gravelly voice called from nearby.

Rhoren stacked the crate he was holding and turned to see the broad-shouldered, gruff glover standing near the front of the wagon, a woman's arm hooked around his. He smoked a pipe with his free hand, blowing smoke to the heavens with each puff. The woman wore a fine dress, sky blue with red roses embroidered about the skirt. Both the shoulders and flounce were full of ruffles, and white lace gloves covered both hands.

"We're getting close." Rhoren placed a hand on the crate. "This is the final ingredient, so to speak. We'll be doing a soft opening soon. You should stop by."

"I'm not one to turn down a good drink." He puffed on his pipe. "This is my wife, Tabitha. I hope Helena hasn't been too much trouble."

"Pleased to meet you." Rhoren nodded. "Helena has been... Well, let's just say she likes her peace and quiet."

"So she says." Tabitha shifted her gaze to the storefront. "I was beginning to think this building would lie empty forever."

Kallum returned from the bar, stepping beside Rhoren. "Rhoren's not one to turn down a good challenge, it seems. Turns out all the place needed was a cat."

Titus and Tabitha shared the same confused expression, and Rhoren found himself unable to control his laughter.

He grabbed the crate on each side and lifted. "We'll let you know when we're open."

Inside, Jinx sat on the bar, watching as Rhoren and Kallum brought in the final crates of alcohol. The bottles clinked as Rhoren set a crate on one of the large oak tables. Soon, it would be surrounded by people enjoying drinks and good conversation.

He took a moment to appreciate how far the place had come. Glassware lined the racks, and kegs of beer sat beneath the bar. A dozen varietals of wine were neatly positioned on the shelves, and in a few days, the chiller would arrive. After all this time, it finally looked like a real bar.

Kallum grinned as he placed his crate next to Rhoren's. "That's the last of it."

Rhoren took a deep breath, inhaling the smell of cinnamon from the sticks centered on the table. "I can't believe it. All of this work, and now we'll finally see what comes of it."

Buying everything the bar needed had completely drained twenty years' worth of savings. Everything that surrounded them would determine the fate of the business going forward. While Kallum had been frugal with most of his own creations, some of the ingredients required for Rhoren's father's recipes had not come cheap.

He still had his monthly pension, but his reserves were gone. While he may never end up destitute, he'd only have one opportunity to honor his father's memory in this fashion.

Kallum squeezed him on the shoulder. "Actually, there's one more thing."

His eyes radiated mischief as he disappeared outside. When Kallum returned, he was carrying a large rectangular object covered with cloth. Whatever it was stretched the width of his outstretched arms.

"Did you commission a painting of me and Jinx?" Rhoren smirked, and the cat jumped on the table at the mention of his name.

"I did one better." He set the bottom of the object on the table with a thud. Whatever it was, it was heavy. "Go on, open it."

Jinx pawed at the cloth as Rhoren slowly removed it, revealing a large slab of stained wood. "Cursed Cocktails" was engraved into the wood, the letters painted a vibrant red. Underneath, there was the image of a cat silhouette walking sideways.

Rhoren stared at it for a long moment.

Kallum's smile faded, and he ran his fingers through

his beard nervously. "I know we never settled on a name, and we can change it if you want, but it seemed fitting considering the history of the building. I just thought that—"

"It's perfect." Rhoren looked into the man's bright blue eyes. "I love it."

Beneath the thick gray beard, Kallum's cheeks flushed.

They spent the next few hours navigating around Jinx as they sorted through the alcohol shipment. When they were finished, the shelves were filled with colorful bottles of spirits and wine.

Rhoren returned to the sign. "What do you say we make it official?"

Kallum grinned. "Let me grab the ladder."

The sign was heavy as Rhoren climbed the ladder with it held between outstretched arms. Kallum stood underneath, holding the ladder steady. It had been much easier removing the previous sign, but at least the hooks were still fitted beneath the balcony.

As Rhoren hooked the first ring, he heard a door open nearby. By the time he'd hung the second ring, Helena was looking up at him with her arms crossed.

Her face was framed by a gable-shaped hood in forest green. Clusters of pearls adorned the edges of the velvet headpiece. "Cursed Cocktails, is it?" She shook her head. "Don't you think that will scare away customers?"

"Not at all, Miss Helena." Kallum smiled broadly. "We'll have you for that."

Helena's mouth hung open like fish in stunned silence, opening and closing several times before she scoffed and turned on her heels without another word. A moment later, the door to The Mad Hatter Boutique slammed shut.

Rhoren climbed down the ladder, grinning. "Must you antagonize her?"

Kallum had the decency to at least look ashamed. "I can't help myself."

"Well, looks like you earned the privilege of inviting her to the opening. We can't have our neighbors hating us on day one, now can we?"

21. WOLFWATER SPRITE

The chiller arrived the next day. Two men carried it into the building, placing the heavy contraption behind the bar. The only problem was that it wasn't working.

"Someone will be by later today to activate the rune." One of the men nestled the chiller in place.

"Is that normal?" Rhoren raised a brow.

It seemed more productive to ship the items already activated, unless they were trying to deter bandits. But even if that were the case, there weren't exactly bandits lurking in the alleyways between the Guild District and Trade District.

The man shrugged. "Not usually, but you never know what's going to happen with gnomes. They can be flighty at times."

"That's an understatement," Kallum mumbled under his breath.

A few hours later, there was a knock at the door. Through the window, Rhoren saw a gnome standing on the tips of her toes, bouncing merrily as she waited outside the door.

She wore goggles that were pushed up to her hairline, and a beautiful plume of magenta hair flowed upward like a flame. Her ears and nose were both rather large, the left ear adorned with several hooped earrings, and she wore a gray robe that had been singed in several areas.

"Hello, Ametrine at your service. I'm here to activate the runes on your chiller." She extended a small hand. "You must be Rhoren."

"Thanks for stopping by." He shook her hand. "Do you normally make house calls?"

Jinx rubbed against Rhoren's leg, eyeing the gnome with intrigue.

"Not usually, but it's not often one has the opportunity to meet a blood mage."

"I'm sorry, what?" Rhoren coughed, looking over his shoulder to where Kallum was cleaning up the area where they had been practicing recipes. "I haven't exactly revealed my role in the Guard to anyone yet."

Her eyes went wide, illuminating the purple irises, before she leaned in and whispered, "I'm sorry. I don't mean to cause a fuss. One of my cousins is a cleric, and he mentioned that there was a—" She mouthed the words 'blood mage.' "—in the city. I've always been fascinated by that type of magic."

"I'm trying to keep a low profile, so I'd appreciate your discretion."

She nodded. "Understood."

"Everything okay over there?" asked Kallum.

"Everything is great." Rhoren's neck tensed as he

turned around. "This is Ametrine. She's here to activate the runes for the chiller."

"Excellent." Kallum clapped his hands together. "Don't let me hold you back."

He moved out of the way so Ametrine would have space to work.

"No need for that." She raised a hand. "It's a simple process really. The devils are in the design. Crafting the rune and channeling mana into the object is the hard part. The activation is basically just flipping the switch."

She pressed her palm to one of the runes. When she removed her hand, the rune glowed a silvery blue. It was composed of nearly a dozen geometric patterns and lines, faintly resembling a snowflake.

When she opened the door to the chiller, a thin layer of frost had already gathered on the inside.

"There we go." Ametrine removed one of the containers from within. "Fill these with water, and you should have ice within a couple of hours." She winked at Rhoren. "Thanks for supporting the Aethervale Guild of Tinkerers, Runecrafters, and Magical Engineers. I'll see myself out."

"Thanks," Rhoren called after her as she was leaving. "Stop by sometime once we're open."

He was sorry that he'd brushed her off, but he still wasn't ready to reveal that part of himself to Kallum—or anyone, really. Maybe in time, but right now, the bar was taking all of his time and energy. If his revelation made Kallum question their partnership, there was no way he could do this alone. His chest felt tight, like a bubble was inflating in his core. The longer he waited, the harder it would be to broach the subject. He'd thought that maybe he could ignore it, but if the gnomes were talking, others would as well.

Jinx climbed inside the chiller, investigating the new addition to the bar.

"Nope." Rhoren grabbed the curious beast around the midsection and pulled him out. "Catsicles are not on the menu."

By early evening, the blocks of ice were frozen solid. Kallum removed one, and chipped a few pieces from the block, nodding approvingly.

"Now the real fun begins." He tossed an ice chip in his mouth. "I wanted to wait until we had ice before I told you, but I've settled on the final cocktail for the menu."

Kallum went over to the table and grabbed Rhoren's journal. He placed it on the bar, face up to the page for the Wolfwater Sprite.

Wolfwater Sprite

Ingredients:

2 oz Jin
1 oz Lime Juice
.75 oz Simple Syrup
3 cucumber slices
8 blueberries
Soda Water

On the page to the left, there was a sketch of a rock formation that resembled a wolf's head. Several fairy-like creatures flew through the air surrounding the rock. His father had even gone so far as to draw one of the creatures sitting on the rim of the glass depicting the cocktail.

Rhoren skipped past the tasting notes to the drink's origin.

In the heart of the Republic of Gannett lies the city of Wolfwater, named after the rock formation that rises from the center of the most tranquil lake I have ever seen. The city rests on one side of the lake, and the other is open wilderness for as far as the eye can see. While Wolfwater lacks the carefree spirit I found along the coast, it has been easy to feel at peace when gazing upon the towering pines in the moonlight.

Legend says that the rock formation is actually Grarra, the Goddess of the Hunt, trapped in her wolf form by the trickster god Nuros. On a moonlit night, some say they can see the forest sprites hovering around the wolf's head as they search for a way to free their patron from her shackles.

The Wolfwater Sprite embodies the atmosphere of the surrounding lake, refreshing and cool like the crisp morning air as the fog peels back from its crystalline surface.

Rhoren smiled as he read the notes. Just reading about Wolfwater Lake eased his tension. His father had a way with words, and a skillful hand both in his writing and art. Rhoren had pored through the journal hundreds of times over the years, reliving his father's travels from city to city across Aedrea. The one thing he'd never understood was why his father had ever decided to return to Hollowton.

Kallum pulled Rhoren from his thoughts when he set a

block of ice on the bar with a thud. "Our shipment of soda water came in yesterday, so we can finally put this one to the test."

Side by side, the two crafted the Wolfwater Sprite. First, Rhoren sliced a cucumber, three slices for himself and three for Kallum. They each added the cucumber, along with lime juice, blueberries, and simple syrup into their shakers.

As they muddled the items, the lime and cucumber made a fragrant aroma that filled the area. Next, they added the jin and then chipped off enough ice to fill the shaker halfway.

They shook the ingredients vigorously. As Rhoren was about to pour the contents into a glass, Kallum held out a hand to stop him.

"This is where we are going to mix it up. There are two ways we can serve it. The first is by pouring the contents directly into the glass. The second is by straining away the muddled berries and cucumber. I say we do one of each and see which one we like better."

"Sounds good to me." Rhoren held out a hand. "Pass me the strainer?"

Kallum emptied the contents of his shaker into the glass while Rhoren carefully strained his. The liquid only filled the bottom third of the glass, so he chipped off fresh ice and dropped it in. The bottle of soda water opened with a hiss, and they topped the cocktails with a generous amount, garnishing the cocktail with a sprig of mint and a slice of cucumber.

Kallum placed his drink next to Rhoren's. "What do you think?"

Even though they were the same drink, the appearance

was a nice contrast. Rhoren's cocktail showcased the light pink color of the muddled blueberries. Kallum's, on the other hand, had blues, pinks, and shades of green. One was elegant, the other chaos.

"I like them both, but we already have other drinks with muddled ingredients. Maybe we strain this one so it stands out."

Kallum nodded. "They taste the same in the end, but you make a good point. Strained it is. Now the best part." He lifted his glass to Rhoren. "To finalizing the menu."

"Cheers to that."

Their glasses clinked, and Rhoren sipped his father's drink for the first time. It was refreshing, crisp, and cool, just like the journal said. The cucumber gave it a subtly sweet element that set it apart from everything else on the menu, and the soda water amplified both the taste and smell of the ingredients as the effervescence tickled his lips.

Rhoren sat back in his chair and let out a deep sigh. There was a sense of relief at finalizing the menu. Somehow, they'd managed to blend the recipes from his father's journal with Kallum's own creations, making something truly special. Nowhere else in Eastborne would people be able to find drinks like this.

Cursed Cocktails was ready to take the city by storm.

22. CALM BEFORE THE STORM

Kallum leaned over the table in the center of the room, writing down the menu on a sheet of parchment. Several drafts lay scattered around the table, the man's perfectionist nature showing in earnest. In a few hours, the doors would open and Cursed Cocktails would be Eastborne's newest business.

Jinx lay sprawled on his back, swatting at the feather quill with each stroke of the pen. He'd caught the quill several times, leaving a streak of ink across the parchment and forcing Kallum to start over. The man's patience was never-ending, however. Occasionally, he would tickle the cat's nose with the feather tip, instigating him into a new round of attacks.

Rhoren sat near the fireplace in one of the oversized leather chairs. It was comfortable, and he stared at the detail in the two giant tapestries that framed the mantle while his mind wandered. The temperature wasn't cool enough to need a fire yet, but he'd been assured that in a few months, the evenings would be crisp enough to get some use out of it.

His foot twitched with nervous energy as he sat there imagining the first customers that would come into the bar. The thought turned his palms sweaty.

"Just what I need for making drinks," he mumbled.

"Talking to yourself again, Rhor?" Kallum set the quill down, and gave the elf a sympathetic look. "First-day jitters are the worst. By this time tomorrow, you'll be an old hand, and the excitement will be back."

"What if no one shows?" Rhoren sat forward, gazing into the empty fireplace as if it held all the answers in the world. "What if I made a mistake by doing all of this?"

"Don't say that." Kallum walked over and tapped Rhoren on the knee. "We've got a good bar here. It will only take one drink for people to realize that. We're building something special, and when our friends and neighbors show up tonight to support us, they'll see it too. Besides, I've hired a crier to shout about us this evening, and I've placed flyers on some of the notice boards." He stared at Rhoren until the elf made eye contact. "People will come."

Rhoren smiled. He wasn't sure how he could have done any of this without Kallum. The man had gone above and beyond, treating every decision with the same respect he would have if it were his own coin at stake.

They'd done everything they could to prepare for tonight. The hard part wasn't the waiting. He'd waited plenty in the Guard. It was the anticipation, the fear of opening the door to an empty street.

"Alright, enough brooding for you." Kallum tapped

him on the leg again. "Let's give you something to do. On your feet. Come tell me what you think of the menu."

Rhoren chuckled as he walked over to the table where Kallum had been working. Charence had always called him a brooder. Rhoren called it introspection, but was there really a difference?

He grinned as he shuffled through Kallum's unsatisfactory attempts. Some had giant Xs while others were crumpled into balls. Rhoren tossed one of the paper balls across the room, and Jinx leapt off the table in pursuit.

Kallum handed one of the unmarked menus to Rhoren. "What do you think?"

He scanned it over. "I never knew you had such good penmanship."

The text was elegantly written and legible, with drink names and brief descriptions of each one.

Cursed Cocktails
Devilishly Delicious Drinks

Eastborne Sour
Rye wuiskey, lemon, simple syrup, red wine float
Tart, with a subtle sweetness

Cogwalloper
Gold rhum, raspberry syrup, lime, orange liqueur
Sweet and refreshing, boozy

Wolfwater Sprite
Jin, lime, simple syrup, cucumber, blueberry, soda water

Refreshingly cool and sweet

Pleasant Peasant
Rhum, lime, sugar
Fresh and citrusy

Nelderland Mule
Watka, lime, ginger beer
Light, sweet, refreshing, with a touch of spice

Blood of the Phoenix
Mezcalium, blood orange, lime, grapefruit, blood orange soda
Well-balanced, sweet, and slightly tart

Ale and wine list available upon request

Stop by the food cart out front for a rotating menu by one of our local vendors

Somewhere in the back of the room, Jinx darted from table to table as he continued his battle with the ball of parchment.

Rhoren smiled as he set the menu down on the table. "It looks great. When you see it all written down like that, it's really something, isn't it?"

Kallum squeezed Rhoren's shoulder. "It really is. I don't know if I have ever been this excited to open a bar. Just focus on one drink at a time and enjoy the experience. It will only be opening night at Cursed Cocktails once."

The hours passed as the two of them prepped the bar. Kallum cut the lemons and limes. Rhoren cleaned the mugs and glassware until they sparkled, and he polished the tables and bar until not a speck of dust remained. With the candles lit and cinnamon sticks placed on every table, a buzz of excitement lingered in the air.

An hour before they were scheduled to open, there was a knock on the door. Dingo waited outside, his cart covered and parked to the left of the porch.

"I don't make it up here often, so I wanted to get here early to set up." He looked past Rhoren and nodded approvingly. "Nice place you've got here."

"Thanks. I've got the first-day jitters, but we're excited to open." He stepped aside, gesturing for Dingo to enter. "Come on in and have a drink."

The man's massive mustache twitched. "Don't mind if I do."

Jinx examined Dingo as he sat at the bar but soon left for more interesting pursuits.

Kallum placed a menu in front of Dingo. "Not sure if Rhoren mentioned it or not, but free drinks for our vendors."

Dingo's eyes flashed with excitement. "I was a little upset at the time, but running into that elf seems better and better by the day."

Kallum winked at Rhoren. "Yeah, my prospects have changed quite a bit since meeting him as well."

After looking over the menu for a minute, Dingo ordered a Cogwalloper. Kallum crafted the drink, adding the ingredients and ice into the shaker. After a vigorous shake, he strained the liquid into a glass and topped it with fresh raspberries.

Dingo stared at the bright-red cocktail for a long moment. "Looks almost too good to drink. Almost." He took a sip, and his eyes closed. He gripped the bar with one hand, and when he opened them, there was a euphoric expression on his face. "Damn." He took another drink. "Damn."

Kallum grinned. "Not too bad, eh?"

"Bad?" He licked the lingering liquid from his mustache. "I didn't know alcohol could taste this good."

Kallum and Dingo made small talk, and as the time grew nearer, a crowd started to gather outside the front door. Rhoren recognized several faces, but there were also a few he hadn't seen before. When he spotted Helena with her hands pressed to the window trying to look inside, he knew they were in for an interesting night. Anticipation settled in his chest. For better or worse, they were about to embark on a new adventure.

The bells from the temple rang through the streets, announcing the new hour, and both Dingo and Rhoren moved toward the door.

"Hold up," called Kallum, and he placed a bottle of amber alcohol on the bar. "This will help take the edge off."

He poured the three of them a shot of wuiskey, imported from the dwarven city of Durendreg. They clinked their glasses together and downed the shot.

Rhoren's stomach warmed and the smokey caramel taste lingered on his tongue. His shoulders relaxed slightly, and after taking a deep breath to steel himself, he opened the door. "Welcome to Cursed Cocktails!"

23. OPENING NIGHT

The night passed in a beautiful blur of chaos. For the first hour, Rhoren worked the bar with Kallum, shaking drinks until his forearms burned from the effort.

When there was a moment of peace, where the chatter of a full bar gave the place a life he'd never imagined, Rhoren leaned against the bar, savoring the occasion. Even without a roaring fire, there was a warmth to the room. Laughter and conversation filled the air, and colorful drinks sparkled like fireflies in the night.

Kallum and Rhoren shared a knowing look, as if to say, 'This is what we've worked for.'

"I'll handle the bar for a bit." Kallum wiped the counter in front of him. "Go and schmooze our guests."

Rhoren nodded, his smile saying everything his words couldn't.

His first stop was Titus and Tabitha, who sat at a table with another couple engaged in conversation.

"You've really outdone yourself." Titus raised his Nelderland Mule as Rhoren knelt beside the table. "We brought a few friends. This is Bernerd and Iria. They make some of the finest jewelry in the kingdom."

Bernerd was a lean man with a narrow jawline, a pencil-thin mustache, and neatly-parted hair. He wore several rings on his fingers, one with a golden lion that caught Rhoren's eye. An emerald amulet encased in gold hung across his chest.

Iria wore a complementary dress in shades of green and gold along with a shimmering pearl necklace and matching earrings. She also had a fair number of bracelets and rings.

"Thanks for coming." Rhoren gestured to their jewelry. "You certainly do amazing work."

Tabitha raised her arm before either of them could respond, showing off an elegant pearl bracelet. "They made this pearl bracelet. Bernerd dives for the pearls himself."

Bernerd laughed. "Too bad I don't know how to work a pick, or I'd mine the jewels too."

Iria tapped him on the arm playfully. "The thought of what a pick might do to those lovely hands of yours terrifies me to the depths of my soul."

He opened his palms as if imagining it himself. "The horror!"

They all burst into laughter. Rhoren thanked them for coming and continued his way around the room.

He talked with Hobbe, an older man with a wispy white beard and the owner of The Wandering Owl, one of Eastborne's most popular breweries. They made arrangements to add a keg of their upcoming lager to the menu.

After a few minutes with Willow and Nobbin, a halfling couple who owned the pottery shop, Pottered

Pieces, Rhoren found Helena sitting in one of the oversized chairs by the fireplace with Jinx curled up in her lap. She stroked the cat with one hand and sipped an Eastborne Sour with the other.

"Glad you could make it, Helena. I'd watch out for Jinx. He can get a bit rowdy."

The fact that he hadn't attacked the silver tassels hanging from her headpiece was a wonder in itself.

She set her drink down and scratched the cat under the chin. "This angel? I don't believe it."

Jinx nuzzled against her touch, and Rhoren found himself at a loss for words. Did Helena have a soft spot for animals?

She looked over her shoulder. "It's good to see all of the noise amounted to something worthwhile in the end."

Rhoren accepted her compliment with a smile, thankful that it was him and not Kallum who had greeted her. He gave Jinx a pet on the head. "Behave yourself."

He found Hewelet and his wife, who were admiring the tapestries framing the fireplace, and thanked them for coming. Then he greeted a few of the other business owners who had stopped by for opening night before making his way over to Cindy, James, and Tomas. The three sat at a table by themselves.

Rhoren could tell that they had gone through considerable effort to clean up for the event. Cindy's dress was free from the dirt stains along the hem, but the edges were still frayed. Both children had their hair combed and styled. Compared to the other guests, there was a noticeable difference in the quality of their clothing, and that was likely the reason why they had the table to themselves, in spite of it being half-empty. Rhoren didn't care and took a moment to visit with them. In the Guard, he'd fought side by side with men from many walks of life. He knew that someone's station had little to do with their character.

"What do you think?" Rhoren asked as he sat down.

Tomas tapped his fingers against his Pleasant Peasant while James and Cindy appeared to be sharing a Wolfwater Sprite and a Blood of the Phoenix.

Their father must have noticed Rhoren's confused expression, because he was quick to comment. "Don't worry, your partner assured me they're both virgin cocktails."

"What's a virgin?" Cindy asked as she sipped her drink.

Tomas nearly choked on his own. "Uh. It's uh, well—" He looked to Rhoren for help.

"It means there's no alcohol in it." He winked at Tomas. "Adults can drink alcohol, but if children do, then it turns their fingers into toes. You wouldn't want that to happen, now would you?"

She scrunched her nose. "Eww, that's gross."

"Good." Tomas took her fingers in his. "Because nobody wants to hold your hand if you have toe-fingers."

Cindy's laughter was like a chime on a breezy day. James just rolled his eyes.

Rhoren looked to the boy. "Are you ready to get to work?"

"He hasn't stopped talking about it since we last met." Tomas smiled at his son.

"Alright then, when you finish your drink, start taking any empty glasses off the tables. Kallum will show you how to clean them behind the bar." He turned to Tomas. "How long before you set sail again?"

Tomas frowned. "Too soon, unfortunately." He leaned forward, gazing intently at Rhoren. "I want to thank you for giving James this opportunity. I believe there's a lot he can learn working somewhere like this."

James scurried around the room, picking up empty glasses. He wore a huge grin as he carried them to the bar with full hands.

"He's a good kid. We'll make sure to keep an eye on them while you're gone." Rhoren stood, gesturing toward the front door. "Dingo has his oyster cart outside. Bread and cheese as well. Eat your fill."

After helping James bus some of the tables, Rhoren spotted Jesper at a table against the far wall. He sat with two women—a female gnome and a female dwarf. They looked entranced as he told a story.

"Quite the ladies' man." Rhoren chuckled to himself as he eavesdropped on the conversation.

"—so there he was, back to the cliff with nothing but jagged rocks and a choppy sea beneath him, with three swords pointed at his throat. And Enagor said, 'Gentlemen, I'll give you one last chance to walk away. No one has to get hurt.'"

Jesper took a swig from his drink and stood as he further illustrated his story. "So there I was, hiding behind the cart and trying to calm the horses as these three bandits attempted to rob my friend and mentor, Enagor Stormrider. I was worried for his safety, so I reached in the wagon for my sword, but Enagor raised a finger, telling me to stand still."

He paused, and as if on cue, the ladies leaned forward.

"All of a sudden, one of the bandits slashed at Enagor. I expected him to call on the lightning, but the mad wizard, he leapt off the cliff." The ladies gasped, and a smirk played on Jesper's lips. "The three bandits crept closer to the edge, unable to believe it themselves, when Enagor flew through the sky on a cloud of mist. He soared over the bandits, landing behind them as soft as a cloud. The mist, it hung in the air, and I could see the terror on the bandits' faces, as if their entire lives were playing out before them and they were wondering where it all went wrong.

"Now, let me tell you, Enagor isn't a vengeful man, so he told them to drop their weapons. With shaking hands, the men released their swords, and they clattered against the pebbled ground. Then Enagor said something that I couldn't quite make out. Probably just giving them a good talking-to, I thought. The bandits all nodded, and then the next thing I knew, a gust of mist blasted them off the cliff-side like leaves in a tempest."

There were shocked expressions, and one of the women clutched at her necklace.

Jesper continued. "I ran to the cliff, unable to believe what Enagor had just done. 'You killed them?' I said, as I looked over the edge, expecting to see their corpses strewn about the rocks. Instead, all three of them were fifty yards at sea, swimming toward shore. Enagor looked at me and shrugged, saying, 'What? They all said they could swim.'"

The ladies cheered and laughed, and Jesper took a bow.

Rhoren clapped as he approached the table. "Enagor Stormrider, now that's a name I haven't heard in a while." He flashed Jesper a mischievous grin. "How is he these days?"

"You're familiar with Enagor?" The color suddenly drained from Jesper's cheeks. "Ladies, this is Rhoren, the esteemed owner of this fine establishment. Would you mind grabbing us another round while I talk to him for a moment?"

They giggled as they walked over to the bar, talking amongst themselves in hushed voices.

"You're good. I'll give you that." Rhoren laughed. "I remember reading about Enagor's exploits. A relatively minor mage, as far as history goes, but very few mages have harnessed the power of the wind as he did."

Jesper blushed. "I spend a lot of my free time at the library. The histories make for great stories and songs, especially the lesser-known ones. I just twist them a bit for my own purposes."

"I won't be the one to rat you out." Rhoren clapped him on the shoulder. "I should probably go help Kallum with the drinks for your captive audience, though. Don't be a stranger. There's no better place to share a story or a song than a good tavern."

"I'll keep that in mind." Jesper grinned. "I'm glad the cat worked out."

Rhoren returned to the bar, where Kallum had a shaker in each hand, arms moving like a tambourine player in the height of the Seventh Day Festival. A cool sheen coated the outside of each shaker when he lowered them to the bar, straining their contents into a glass one at a time.

"Miss me?" Rhoren asked as he took the next order, a Blood of the Phoenix for one of Jesper's adoring fans.

Kallum slid the drink across the bar to a guest. "Miss you? I haven't even had time to think about you."

The guest dropped a few coins in the tip jar as he took his drink.

Rhoren added the grapefruit juice to the shaker. "We've had a better turnout than I expected. Even a few new faces."

Kallum laughed. "Free booze will do that." He stopped working and looked over to the door. "Well, I'll be damned."

Rhoren looked up, equally surprised to see Darvish Goldhammer standing in the doorframe and taking the space in. Rhoren waved to the dwarf, and Darvish made his way over to the bar.

The crowd parted before the head of Goldhammer Enterprises as the portly dwarf approached. His thick black beard jingled with each step, golden clasps announcing his every move. Two of his personal guards stood sentry at the doorway.

Darvish looked around, appraising the tavern. "I'm beginning to think I was swindled." There was a long silence before he burst into a deep belly laugh that carried over the crowded room. "You've certainly done right by this place." He grabbed a menu, tracing it with a finger as he skimmed the items. "I'll have one of your, what is it, ah yes, the boozy one, Cogwalloper."

"Coming right up." Kallum rinsed the shaker and started on the next drink.

"Timofey can't be happy losing you, now can he?" Darvish narrowed his eyes. "You've been a staple at the Seaside Inn for years."

Kallum shrugged. "What's life without a little risk?"

"That's the truth of it. Judging by the crowd tonight, it

seems you've hitched your wagon to a good horse with this one."

"I like to think so." Kallum lifted the shaker overhead but then paused. "Speak of the devil and he shall appear."

Darvish looked over his shoulder. "Timofey, you old bastard. Not half as bad as you seem, are you?"

Timofey smiled at his old friend. He wore a purple silk shirt with a button undone that revealed the top of his chest. Rhoren had always admired the man's style. He could somehow blend high society with the carelessness of a wanderer.

The room took notice as he strolled toward the bar, his hair like a fiery beacon as he nodded approvingly.

He placed a hand on Darvish's shoulder, wagging his eyebrows at Kallum before winking at Rhoren. "I assure you, I am worse than I seem by tenfold."

Darvish rumbled with laughter. "You sly demon, sit down and have a drink."

Timofey pulled a stool next to Darvish. "I'll have whatever he's having."

"My pleasure." Kallum grinned. "Thanks for coming. It means a lot."

"It's the least I can do to support someone who has made my life a hell of a lot easier these past few years."

Darvish tilted his head. "I'm surprised you let him get away, to be honest."

"Who am I to stop a flower from blossoming?" He smirked. "If anyone deserves success, it's Kallum. And judging by the look of this place, he might have found it."

Darvish snapped his fingers, and his assistant rushed over. "Go and bring us some oysters. I want the full experience."

The dwarf chatted with Kallum and Timofey while Rhoren lost himself in the process of crafting drinks. He was nowhere near as talented as Kallum, who could hold a conversation as he made two drinks at once, but it had been getting easier. Some of the cocktails he had completely committed to memory and no longer needed to follow the recipe step by step.

As the drinks continued to flow, the atmosphere shifted. Laughter and chatter became a dull roar, and at one point the entire room joined in a verse of *Lady in the Lake*. Even though they were serving refined drinks in a nicer part of the city, it felt like one of the small-town taverns after a long day's work.

Rhoren imagined his father in a place like this, sitting at a table in the corner with a drink in one hand and a pen in the other. All of the fear and anxiety that had swelled inside of Rhoren over the past few months extinguished. He had set sail and was now at the mercy of the winds.

He took a large ale mug and beat it on the counter until he had everyone's attention. Dozens of eyes fell on Rhoren, and he met many of them. The silence was near absolute, save the crackle of candle flame and the distant noise of wagons upon the street.

Rhoren cleared his throat as he stepped onto a stool, giving himself a better look across the room. "Friends, neighbors,—" He grinned as he made eye contact with a balding man holding a cocktail in each hand. "—strangers looking for free drinks. I want to thank you all for coming out tonight. When I moved to Eastborne, I didn't know what to expect. I was a stranger in a strange land, far from home. What I've found here is beyond anything I could have imagined. I sought out the crisp, clean air and the warmth of the sun—" He paused as he found his friends among the crowd, and finally turned to Kallum. "—but what I found was a sense of purpose and a full heart." He pressed his palms together and bowed. "Thank you."

Several fists beat against the tables, and a few howls erupted from the back.

Kallum lifted a bottle of rhum into the air. "To Rhoren. To Cursed Cocktails—"

Jinx leapt onto the bar with a loud meow.

"And to Jinx," Rhoren added, and laughter filled the air.

And the drinks continued to flow.

24. NOT A CROWD IN SIGHT

If opening night had been a tempest, then the next day was calm water.

The excitement of the previous evening had died down, and the realization that they were an upstart business with no name recognition and no clientele lingered like an unwelcome guest. The tavern remained empty for the first few hours. The polished wood and glassware practically sparkled as Kallum and Rhoren kept themselves busy during the downtime.

Now, a single customer sat near the fireplace smoking a pipe and reading a thick leather-bound book. His presence alone had eased much of the tension, a tipping point that said just maybe things would work out.

The man had a wizened look about him. A white beard draped over his chest, and his eyebrows looked like thick gray caterpillars. He puffed his pipe, blowing smoke from his nostrils like a dragon, which had left the thick white mustache stained with a strip of brown over the years.

Occasionally, the man would mutter something before shaking his head and gazing off into the distance.

Jinx lay sprawled at the man's feet, his chest rising and falling as tiny snores punctuated the silence.

Rhoren delivered an Eastborne Sour to the man, placing it on the table next to his chair. The man grunted in acknowledgement but didn't look up from his book.

As Rhoren walked back, he massaged his aching forearms. All the practice in the world hadn't prepared him for the sheer number of drinks he'd made the night before.

"You'll get used to it." Kallum smiled as he rinsed out the shaker and set it on the bar. "Even I'm feeling it a bit after last night."

"It's not that bad." Rhoren flexed his fingers, feeling the sore muscles with every movement.

He enjoyed this type of soreness. It was a discomfort born from hard work, proof that his body was working. Compared to the burning joints and lingering pain that accompanied his blood magic, this was a minor annoyance. Given the choice between the two, he'd take sore muscles a hundred times over.

"Preposterous!" the old man exclaimed, followed by a thud as he slammed the book shut.

Rhoren raised an eyebrow. "Everything okay?"

"Certainly not!" The man stood, startling Jinx, who bolted across the bar with a disgruntled meow. "Imbeciles, the whole lot of them." He sneered at the book that sat in the chair. "Anyone with half a mind can see that bypassing the mountain path is a terrible idea. The dwarves abandoned the mines for a reason."

Rhoren covered his mouth to conceal his smile. "Must be a pretty good book to elicit such a strong reaction."

"It is infuriating! I'd be within my rights to toss it in the fire." He huffed.

"Is that so?" Kallum stepped out from behind the bar. "Hand it here. I can save you the trouble."

"Well, uh—" The man stammered as his eyes fell on the book. "—let's not be hasty." He picked it up, holding it much more gently than before. "I might as well see how it ends."

"Endings are a reward in themselves. Only then can you look back on the journey." Rhoren ran a rag across the already gleaming table. "How'd you find out about us, Mr.—"

"Lostwick. Professor Lostwick, actually. I saw the crowd last night on my way home from the university. I'm not one for large gatherings but your sign intrigued me, so here I am."

"You picked a good time, Professor." Kallum tossed his towel over one shoulder and leaned back against the bar, spreading his arms wide as he gestured around the room. "Not a crowd in sight."

The professor took a drink of the Eastborne Sour. "I don't imagine that will last long. Quite the drink you have here."

Rhoren took a seat in one of the chairs across from the man. "So you're a professor?"

"Currently. I'm only teaching one course, but this is my last semester." The man set the book on the table and chuckled. "Though that's what I've been saying for the last ten years."

Rhoren matched his grin. "You must love it, then."

"Love, hate, there's a fine line between the two." Lost-wick shrugged. "Growing up, I always had an unquenchable thirst for knowledge. When I started university, I realized that I never wanted to leave, so I didn't. My family wasn't too happy about that, but it's hard to walk away from your calling. Truth be told, I'll probably die at the podium."

"That'll be a lecture they'll never forget." Kallum laughed. "What is it you teach?"

"Mythical creatures. Their histories, origins, and how to find them."

Kallum joined them around the fireplace. "Now, that is fascinating. I'd love to hear how a professor in a large city knows how to find mythical creatures."

"I save that knowledge for the lecture field study." Lostwick gave Kallum a mischievous look. "Unfortunately, class is full this semester."

"Forbidden knowledge." Kallum waggled his brows. "How enticing! Maybe a few drinks will loosen those lips."

"You are welcome to try, my dear boy."

The door opened, and James hurried inside, out of breath. He leaned forward, heaving with his hands on his knees. "Sorry, I'm late! There was an overturned cart blocking the bridge. I ran as fast as I could after it cleared."

"No worries." Rhoren winked at the boy. "Looks like you're right on time to me."

"Yeah, not much going on at the moment." Kallum grabbed a broom from behind the bar. "Why don't you sweep the porch after you catch your breath?"

James grinned as he took the broom. A few minutes

later, his whistles could be heard from outside as he swept.

"I wonder how long that will last?" asked Kallum.

"People can appreciate anything if it gives them purpose." Rhoren peeked through the window, watching the boy. James had changed a great deal since their first encounter. Then, he'd been timid and distrustful, constantly on the edge of fighting or fleeing. A little kindness had softened him around the edges, but now he was morphing again. He nodded to people as they passed, no longer looking to become invisible.

As the day wore on, customers filtered in. A young couple came, arms intertwined as they ordered their drinks, followed by a merchant. Professor Lostwick stayed for a while longer, muttering to himself as he read.

The food cart for the evening sold hot meat pies, and the savory aroma drifted inside every time the door opened.

More than once, hands pressed against the window as passersby peeked inside before going elsewhere. The location in the Trade District meant that there were always people around. The challenge was luring them inside. After the evening bell, a couple of tables filled, and while they were never at full capacity, there was enough business to keep them busy, including James.

After closing for the day, Rhoren called the boy over. He pulled a silver coin from his pocket and pressed it against James's palm. "Good work today. Kallum and I will finish up for the night."

James's eyes went wide as he held the coin. In most taverns, three meals a day and a bed were all the payment a kid might receive. If they were lucky, they might earn a copper a day, two if the owner was generous. This kind of coin would go a long way for the Crookshank family. It was probably a lot closer to what Tomas earned than either of them would like to admit.

"Sir…" James's eyes glistened.

Rhoren held up a hand. "Go on home. We'll see you tomorrow."

James gripped the coin like it might escape.

As he left, Kallum looked up from his work at the bar, where he was keeping record of the drinks they'd sold. "That was nice of you."

"He earned it. Why shouldn't he be compensated at a fair rate for the work?"

Kallum's lip curled at the edge. "I'm not arguing with you. It's just not a common way of doing business. Too often, it's profits over people."

Rhoren took a seat at the bar across from Kallum. "It might not be common, but I like to think that if you pay fair wages and treat your employees with respect, then maybe they won't be tempted to open a bar with the first umbral elf that walks into town."

"You've certainly got me there." Kallum laughed. "You might be better suited to own a business than you realize."

Rhoren leaned forward, glancing down at the parchment. "How'd we do?"

"Not too bad for our first real day. We couldn't cover rent at this rate, but since you own the building, that's one less thing to consider. Usually, it takes a few months to build up regulars." He turned the parchment to face Rhoren, showing him the tally of the day's drinks. "It's a small sample size, but the Eastborne Sour seems to be the most popular cocktail so far. Could be the name of the drink or its prominence at the top of the menu that's appealing to people. For non-cocktails, ale sells better than wine, but again, it's a small sample."

Rhoren looked over the data. "You managed to do all of this while making drinks?"

"We weren't exactly swarmed." He grinned. "If you want to run a successful business, it's important to keep a list of everything. Say what you will about Timofey, but the man keeps excellent records."

Rhoren walked behind the bar, taking a bottle of watka shipped from the human city of Silverpeak. The label depicted a falcon sitting on a mountain peak. He poured himself and Kallum two knuckles worth of the clear alcohol, and then chipped two large pieces of ice from the block.

The glass tinkled as he sat it in front of Kallum. "To doing things the right way."

They clinked their glasses together and drank. The chilled alcohol cooled Rhoren's throat, and then warmed his belly. Silverpeak was known for using some of the coldest water in the realm when distilling watka, pulling it straight from their mountain springs. It resulted in a liquor that was smooth and pure with notes of vanilla, white pepper, and cream.

"That's good." Kallum sniffed the drink before setting it on the bar, staring at it contemplatively before meeting Rhoren's gaze. "It might be slow starting out, but you've really got a good thing here."

"No." Rhoren shook his head. "We've got a good thing here. I couldn't do any of this without you."

"I wouldn't be so sure about that." Kallum winked. "You're a natural behind the bar."

Compared to Kallum, Rhoren always felt he was one step behind, but it boosted his confidence to hear the man's words. After they finished their drinks, he rinsed the glasses and wiped down the bar a final time.

They'd survived their first full day in business, and tomorrow, they'd do it all again.

25. EASTBORNE DINNER CULT

The coming weeks were slow for business, but they quickly settled into routine for Kallum and Rhoren. The duo worked the bar together five evenings a week, with each taking one day off while the other worked a solo shift. Since Rhoren lived above the bar, he often found himself downstairs even on his scheduled day off.

Not that he complained. Cursed Cocktails had provided him with purpose and excitement that fulfilled him like no other. With each new day, the drinks poured a little quicker than the day before until he could almost keep pace with Kallum. Every drink further cemented his father's memory and was a brick in the foundation of his own legacy. He'd made a name for himself as the Bloodbane. Perhaps now he could forge a new one as Rhoren Balsalor, son of Dhorian.

Maintaining records and taking inventory were all part of the day's work, and Rhoren grew to enjoy every bit of it. The life of a bar owner suited him, and if

Charence ever made his way south, he'd make sure the cleric had all the drinks he could handle.

Rhoren found himself working alone on Ydden, which was always one of the slower days as everyone returned to work. He felt confident enough to hold the bar down with a little help from James. Even though Rhoren occasionally woke in a cold sweat from nightmares filled with endless customers and spilled drinks, nothing had come close to the chaos of opening night.

He stood behind the bar as the last bit of sunlight disappeared outside the window. A handful of customers sat scattered around the room. Titus and his wife, who had become regulars, shared a platter of oysters at the far table, while a young man savored a glass of wine as he read through a scroll in front of the fireplace. Two gnomes drank Cogwallopers as they played a board game at the closest table, laughing and bickering as they moved pieces across a checkered piece of wood.

The door opened, and heavy footsteps thudded against the floor as a tall, broad-shouldered man entered. He wore a dark green cloak with a hood that covered most of his face. The cloak was wool, fine quality but well-worn, stained in places and frayed at the edges from heavy use. An assortment of holes revealed the boiled leather armor hidden underneath. Most might not notice the outline of a dagger and sword gently bulging against each hip, but Rhoren had enough experience in that regard. The man's boots were well-traveled, and Rhoren pegged him as a ranger, possibly an adventurer.

A dozen questions ran through the elf's mind. In his months since calling Eastborne home, he'd learned that encountering an adventurer this far south was nearly as rare as seeing a mage. They'd come to the city for jobs or to collect bounties, stopping by the Adventurers' Guild for quests that lay far beyond the reach of the city watch.

The man pulled back the hood of his cloak, revealing a fiery beard and a hawk-like nose. Green eyes as lush as spring grass scanned the room in an instant before lingering on Rhoren.

"I need a drink. Something strong." The man tapped his coin pouch and it jingled.

"We've got strong drinks, all right." Rhoren pointed to the menu laying on the bar.

The man frowned as he read it over. "Gods be damned, don't you have ale?"

Generally, adventurers gravitated toward taverns with strong ale and rowdy patrons, which was all the more confusing as to why one was in the Trade District.

"We've got ale—some of the best in the realm from Barrowsturm to Rakroft—but we offer drinks you can't find anywhere else in Eastborne. The recipes come from all over Aedrea, passed down to me from my father on his travels."

The man looked up curiously. "Your pops was an adventurer?"

Rhoren grinned, knowing he had judged him right. "Not in the same sense as you, but he had an adventurous spirit."

"Alright, you've convinced me." He pushed the menu forward. "But like I said, something strong."

"Coming right up." Rhoren grabbed the rhum and started work on the Cogwalloper, making small talk as he crafted the drink. "What brings you to Eastborne?"

The man looked over his shoulder before returning his

attention to Rhoren. "Special business. I have an appointment with a nobleman, and if I don't have a drink before I go, I'm likely to show him the pointy end of my sword."

"That bad?" Rhoren gave the man his attention as he added ice to the shaker.

"Oh, you know the kind. They think the world revolves around them and the rest of us are lucky to be in their presence."

"This should help with that." Rhoren winked as he added a little extra rhum to the shaker. After vigorously shaking, Rhoren strained the contents into a glass. "Why do you do it then?" He asked the question, but he already knew the answer.

The man tapped his coin pouch again. "I follow the coin, and I can count on this lot to fill my purse at least once a season."

Rhoren finished the deep-red cocktail with a garnish of raspberries and slid it across the bar. "Work is work. I'm not one to bemoan anyone making an honest living."

"Cheers to that!" The adventurer lifted his glass, tapped it to the bar in a show of respect, and took a hardy drink, draining the cocktail in one motion. The man blinked rapidly as he set the glass back on the bar. "By the gods, that's good. One more for the road."

"Be careful." Rhoren rinsed the shaker and prepared to make another. "Those things are stronger than they look."

"That's what they say about me." The man winked.

"You look pretty strong already." Rhoren had found out long ago that flattery worked wonders on adventurers.

"Exactly." He smirked as the alcohol began to take effect. "I've traveled all across Aedrea in my time.

Whether it be man, woman, or monster, Dobbin has yet to find a foe he couldn't match."

"I believe it. Dobbin, is it? You can call me Rhoren."

Dobbin nodded his acknowledgment and sipped the second Cogwalloper a little slower, savoring the taste. "This is a nice place you have here, Rhoren. I don't remember seeing it last time I was in Eastborne. Just so happens I saw that fellow over there drinking his wine as I was walking down the street."

"We've only been open for a few weeks now, but it's good to know we at least look appealing."

"Here's to hoping you stick around." Dobbin raised his glass and pointed over his shoulder. "What's with the Northern Guard tapestry? You don't see those much this far south."

Rhoren's gaze settled on the tapestry depicting the crest of the Northern Guard over a snowy mountain range. "I served before I moved here."

"You don't say?" Dobbin shifted in his seat excitedly. "I served in the Warminster military in my younger years. Adventuring is a lot more fun."

Rhoren laughed. "I do not doubt it."

A second drink quickly turned into a third, and Dobbin boasted about some of his adventures, sharing stories with Rhoren from his time in the military. By the time he finished, there was a slight glaze to his eyes.

He leaned forward, looking over each shoulder to make sure no one was lurking. "Want to know a secret?"

Rhoren leaned closer, matching the man's enthusiasm. "Always."

"There's a secret society among the nobles of East-borne," he whispered. "They call themselves the Eastborne

185

Dinner Cult. A few times a year, they hire me to hunt down rare or magical creatures so that they can eat them."

Rhoren wore a shocked expression. "And what, they just eat rare creatures?"

Dobbin nodded. "They believe it brings them closer to the gods."

"Oh, wow. What do you usually bring them?"

"Whatever they want, if the coin is good. Fairies. Wargs. Last year, I traveled all the way to Drake Canyon for slimes. That one took me half the year." He frowned so hard that it was almost a snarl. "Who knows what the bastard will ask for this time."

"You keep coming back, so it must not be all bad."

Dobbin tried to take a drink from the empty glass. When nothing came out, he sighed. "I guess that's my cue. I'll be in town for a few days at least. I'll stop back by and try some of your other offerings." He reached in his pocket, pulling out a handful of silver coins and letting them fall on the counter. "Will this cover it?"

Rhoren laughed. "See you around, Dobbin."

Dobbin grinned as Rhoren slid the coins off the bar.

Even before owning a bar, Rhoren could tell the difference between a good adventurer and a great one. A good adventurer would count their coin as they paid; a great one didn't need to.

The remaining customers slowly filtered out, allowing Rhoren and James to clean the tables and mop the floor. Jinx pounced on the mop as it sloshed across the ancient wood. Upon discovering it was wet, the cat bolted up the stairs, leaving a trail of wet pawprints in his wake.

After paying James for his work, Rhoren filed away the day's records and locked the coins in a chest upstairs. The moon cast a silver glow upon the balcony, and a hooting owl could be heard through the open window.

Rhoren climbed into bed, wondering what other interesting people he might meet in the days ahead. There was a gentle pressure as Jinx leapt onto the bed, followed by a warm nuzzle as the massive cat plopped into the crook of Rhoren's arm.

26. A DISAPPEARANCE

A loud thud woke Rhoren from a peaceful slumber. He sat up, hands resting on the blanket where Jinx had been curled up when he fell asleep. The spot was still warm.

"What are you into now?" Rhoren mumbled.

Jinx's presence had been enough to ward off any visiting vermin, and over time, the cat had taken to sleeping in the bed with Rhoren. The only disturbances nowadays were when Jinx inexplicably darted across the room for no reason or attacked Rhoren's feet as he shifted in his sleep.

The cat was a mischief-maker with a penchant for knocking things over, so Rhoren groaned as he crawled out of bed. He'd rather deal with the situation now than accidentally step on broken glass in the morning.

Cool night air spilled in from the open window, causing the curtain to flutter in the moonlight. Rhoren wrapped a blanket over his shoulders and made his way downstairs to survey the damage.

He expected to find the cat standing over a broken bottle or some other object he'd knocked to the floor. Instead, all Rhoren found was emptiness. He checked the fireplace, where Jinx would often curl up in one of the oversized chairs, then behind the bar, where the cat would sometimes cram into nooks that he should not have been able to fit into. Rhoren opened all of the drawers and cabinets, even the chiller, as he searched for the rogue feline.

Through it all, there was no trace of Jinx. Both doors were shut and locked with no evidence of forced entry.

Rhoren called for Jinx to no response, so he went back upstairs, checking underneath the bed and every other cranny that might conceal the giant cat.

His gaze fell upon the door to the balcony, and a sense of unease settled in his stomach. Jinx would often lie on the balcony during the day, basking in the warmth of the sun. Even though Rhoren was certain the noise had come from downstairs, he still leaned over the rail, looking into the street below. There was nothing but empty streets and flickering lamps.

"What in the hells?" Rhoren rubbed his brow. It was as if the cat had just vanished.

He returned downstairs, scanning the room again as his mind raced with possibilities of where the cat could be hiding. He called for Jinx over and over, even rattling the container that held the cat's treats. That action alone would normally produce the patter of feet from wherever Jinx might be lurking about.

Wearing only his night clothes and a blanket, Rhoren stepped into the street, walking the perimeter of the building and catching a confused look from a city guard patrolling the square. If Jinx had jumped from the balcony, he was nowhere to be found.

Back inside, Rhoren crawled on hands and knees into the fireplace to see if Jinx had tried to climb the chimney. The grate they'd added to keep out animals was still intact. Feeling defeated, he sat in one of the chairs and massaged his eyes with open palms.

Rhoren sighed. There was still one way to find Jinx if he was hiding somewhere on the property.

He clenched his fists and only the faintest tingle flared within his joints. That option would be a last resort. Rhoren had searched everywhere he could. If Jinx had found a way out, then he hoped that the cat had enough sense to find his way back in.

With a sinking pit in his stomach, Rhoren returned to bed with the hope that Jinx would return by the time he woke. Except sleep didn't come easy. The mystery of Jinx's disappearance gnawed at him like a wolf over a carcass in the dead of winter. It wasn't like Jinx to disappear. If anything, the cat had gotten clingier. The noise. The still-warm bed. Something didn't add up.

"To hells with it." Rhoren sat up and rubbed his hands together, mentally preparing for what was about to happen.

He closed his eyes and focused, activating his blood sense.

Rhoren's body tensed as his magic took hold. He tried to block out the searing veins as the thousands of heartbeats of men, women, and animals overwhelmed him, far denser than anything he'd experienced in the Guard. So dense that the outlines he would normally see blended together in a maelstrom of pulsing veins. Stars danced behind his closed eyelids, and the cacophony of beating hearts thundered in his mind as his perception stretched for hundreds of feet in all directions.

He breathed slowly, regaining control and narrowing his perception. Thousands of heartbeats faded to hundreds. He narrowed it further to less than thirty feet out, but that still produced dozens of results. The slow rhythmic pulse of a couple sleeping. The lone heartbeat next door that belonged to Helena. An owl perched somewhere overhead, and rodents moved through the alleys. A myriad of creatures crawled the streets at night.

Then he noticed something strange. Two heartbeats, definitely not human, coming from below. Not downstairs, but further down, deep underground.

Rhoren opened his eyes, his own heartbeat thundering like a hammer and anvil. Perspiration covered his forehead, and his knuckles flared white from gripping the blanket. As he moved out of bed, his knees buckled. He had to lean against the wall for support as he descended the stairs.

At the bottom of the stairs, Rhoren sat, activating his blood sense again and fighting the urge to scream as he focused on the two beating hearts below. He couldn't be sure that one of them belonged to Jinx, but he knew they were relatively small animals. He could see their outline in his mind's eye. If only he'd used his blood sense before now, then he'd be able to recognize Jinx among the chaos.

Rhoren opened his eyes again, this time retching into a bucket behind the bar. His entire being shook from the effort as what had been commonplace not even a year ago now drained him to his core. It was as if any tolerance he had to the effects of blood magic had faded away from disuse.

As he sat there, regaining his composure, he recalled his encounter with the alchemist across the river. She'd mentioned catacombs that ran beneath the city, ancient tunnels that had been used for transport at one point. It was the only plausible explanation for Jinx's disappearance, but that meant there had to be an access point within the building. None of his research before buying the property detailed anything like that.

Haunted buildings, mysterious noises, it all suddenly made sense, but who or what was behind them remained to be seen.

Rhoren dropped to his hands and knees, poking and prodding at every plank of wood. Not knowing exactly what he was searching for, he focused like a hunter on the trail, looking for anything out of the ordinary—a crack in the floor, a wobbly floorboard. If there was a secret entrance, it was well-hidden, so much so that none of the previous inhabitants had stumbled upon it.

He quickly resolved that it was unlikely to be in the floorboards, and by the time the sun was peeking through the window, he'd determined that there were no loose planks in the wall either.

Maybe he'd been wrong. Maybe there was no secret entrance into the catacombs. It was possible that the heartbeats he'd located were wild animals hunting in the ruins of ages past.

His gut argued otherwise. If Jinx had found a way out, then it meant one of two things. Either the access point was low enough to the ground that a cat could reach it, or it had been opened from the other side. Rhoren knelt, running his fingers along the baseboard trim that ran the perimeter of the room. He started behind the bar and worked his way to the stairs. When he pressed the baseboard beneath the stairwell, there was a faint give. It was almost imperceptible but when he pressed it harder, something clicked. A few feet away, a piece of the wall swung open, bumping against one of the tables.

"I'll be damned." Rhoren stood, his discomfort replaced with a childlike sense of wonder.

He moved the table a few feet over and opened the secret door, revealing a dusty stone stairwell that led deep underground. A musty smell drifted up from below.

There was almost no light, but the elf's above-average dark vision was enough to make out the features. At the bottom of the stairwell, Jinx lay curled in a ball. He raised his head, meowing at Rhoren.

"How did you get down there?"

Rhoren took a step into the stairwell and froze. A black tail with a blueish-white tip appeared from behind Jinx. A gentle glow surrounded the tail, and a mound of black fur shifted.

Jinx wasn't alone.

Two glowing blue eyes stared at Rhoren as a spirit fox stretched its legs.

27. GUARDIAN OF THE NIGHT

The fox stared at Rhoren from the bottom of the stairwell, its three tails swishing as Jinx nuzzled against the mythical creature. The fox was a shadowy black, but each tail was tipped in an ethereal blue that produced a soft glow in the dark tunnel.

Rhoren was at a loss. Had this been the creature sneaking into his building, eating the cheese, and dismantling the traps? Was it responsible for the deserted storefronts time and again?

The ramblings of the disfigured man in the alchemist colony repeated in his mind. *"Beware the guardian of the night. She watches. Always watching."*

Had the man known? The alchemists hadn't used the catacombs for transport in many years—not since the explosion that had leveled a city block, but that didn't mean they were abandoned.

Rhoren recalled his conversation with Hewelet at the tapestry shop. He'd said that spirit foxes were a Nelderland legend, creatures said to watch over the dead and keep evil spirits at bay.

Were they real? Rhoren had asked while looking at the tapestry, as if spirit foxes were somehow less believable than behemoths and dragons. The proof of their existence was before him now.

Rhoren knelt, a hand outstretched to call Jinx, when he noticed a lever on the inside of the wall to his left. It sat a few inches off the ground, and when he toggled the apparatus, a mechanism moved inside the frame of the hidden door. Maybe Jinx hadn't escaped. The lever took a great deal less effort to open the door than pressing the baseboard on the other side, and it was possible for a paw to activate the switch. Perhaps the spirit fox had opened the door.

Rhoren tested the mechanism. The door opened with a gentle click, but when it shut, there was a loud thud.

The fox watched Rhoren intently while Jinx continued his affectionate nuzzling.

Rhoren extended his hand, rubbing his fingers together to entice the cat. When that didn't work, he went back inside and returned with the container of treats.

Both cat and fox ears perked up when Rhoren rattled the container. His fingers ached as he removed two slices of the mysterious jerky meat. The animals sniffed at the air as the smell drifted down. Jinx ascended the stairs, but the spirit fox was more hesitant, taking a few steps and stopping.

Jinx placed both of his large front paws on Rhoren's knees and snatched the jerky. Rhoren inched forward, holding out the second piece toward the fox.

"It's okay. I'm not going to hurt you," he said as calmly

as he could. The spirit fox tilted its head and climbed one of the stairs. "There you go. Come and get it."

The process took several minutes, but the fox crept closer until it was an arm's length away. Rhoren leaned closer and the fox took the meat, darting down the stairs and into the darkened catacombs.

Rhoren looked to Jinx, who stood beside him watching the fox's glowing tails. "Might as well explore while we have the chance."

Jinx meowed in response, rubbing against Rhoren's leg.

Rhoren grabbed a lamp from behind the bar and descended the stairs. The dull light revealed the immediate area, but darkness pervaded in all directions, save the gentle glow from the fox's tails. Smooth stone floors were covered in a layer of dust and dirt, and cobwebs draped the walls and ceiling. While the passage wasn't narrow, a single wagon could only travel one way unimpeded. Empty sconces adorned the walls, and smaller passages only wide enough for foot traffic disappeared into the underground labyrinth.

Who knew what ancient secrets lay hidden within?

Jinx and the fox rubbed heads, and the spirit fox approached Rhoren with caution. He tossed another piece of jerky to the fox, who devoured the aged meat, so Rhoren grabbed another piece and knelt, holding it out as an offering. The fox was hesitant as it approached.

It took the meat from his trembling fingers, still shaking from the toll of blood magic. This time, the fox only retreated a few feet away. Rhoren repeated the gesture two more times, until the fox ate the jerky right in front of him. He reached out and stroked the animal's silky-smooth fur. The spirit fox watched him for a moment, but then returned to its meal.

After finishing, the fox placed its front paws on Rhoren's knees in a similar manner to how Jinx did when he begged for more.

"You must be hungry down here." He gave the fox the last of the treats. "Consider this an apology for me trying to murder you."

Jinx pawed at one of the fox's tails as she ate. The fact that the cat and fox hadn't tried to kill one another likely meant that the fox was female. Rhoren placed his hands on the ground to get a better look, and a shooting pain flared through his wrists.

After his suspicions were confirmed, Rhoren massaged his hands, wondering how he was going to explain any of this to Kallum.

"What do you say we take a look around?" he asked neither animal in particular, but as he walked further into the catacombs, both creatures followed.

The tunnel led in the direction of the higher districts, where the keep sat behind closed gates. There were dozens of passageways, and these underground corridors likely stretched all over the city.

They came upon a section of tombs where skeletons still rested within. The alchemists had used the tunnels to transport dangerous chemicals, but long before that, the catacombs were tombs for the dead. Some of the bones were wrapped in long-decayed bandages that were nothing more than tatters. Others had been moved or rearranged. Broken stone lay scattered about from where the tombs had been opened, the inscription of their inhabitants faded with time. One of the passageways had been blocked with a barricade of stacked skulls. Hundreds of tombs stretched along the corridor for as far as the lamp would shine.

There was a peacefulness to the silence of the catacombs. Each footstep stretched for infinity. Somewhere out of sight, water dripped rhythmically. It reminded Rhoren of his treks into the wilderness, where snow concealed everything that wasn't right before him.

"A guardian of the dead, huh?" He watched the fox as she walked ahead.

Certain creatures were drawn to particular habitats. Some fae preferred the depths of ancient forests. Elemental spirits were drawn to water or fire. Was the spirit fox drawn to the dead?

According to Hewelet, spirit foxes were symbols of good. If the legends were true, then the presence of one kept wraiths, specters, and the undead at bay. The irony that she was the reason people thought the building was haunted brought a smile to Rhoren's face.

He could have spent the entirety of the day exploring the underbelly of Eastborne, but his joints had other ideas and complained with every move he made. He wasn't sure how or if he could explain this to Kallum, but if he was going to work tonight, then he needed the day to rest.

28. HALF-KEPT SECRETS

"You look like death." Kallum placed a hand on Rhoren's shoulder as he stepped inside. "Was the shift that bad?"

"Couldn't sleep," Rhoren lied. Even though his solo shift was only the previous night, it felt like days had passed since he'd worked the bar. He'd slept the majority of the day away since returning from the catacombs, and his body still ached. His muscles were sore, his joints burned, and his head pounded worse than any hangover he'd ever experienced. "The shift wasn't too bad. I met an adventurer who hunts rare meat for something called the Eastborne Dinner Cult."

"Really?" Kallum wore an amused expression, petting Jinx as the cat nuzzled against his leg. "I always thought that was a myth. I guess there's a little truth in everything."

Rhoren's mind went back to the spirit fox. "I guess so."

Kallum set a small crate of lemons and limes on the counter. "We're going to be busy this weekend. It's the start of the Storm Festival."

"Storm Festival?" Rhoren raised a brow. "What's that?"

"Oh, right. I guess it's only a Nelderland tradition. The Storm Festival is supposed to bring in the rainy season and bless the farmlands with a bountiful crop. All of the towns and villages have one, but Eastborne's is the biggest outside of Tiberia. People come from all over to see it, and there's a parade that ends with a firelight display. People dress up in costume to honor the gods, and the streets are filled with people drinking and eating." Kallum grinned. "It's a glorious time."

"Sounds like it." Rhoren laughed. "I've heard of fire-lights used for entertainment, but in the Guard, they were only used as emergency signals. A bright red trail of light would shoot high into the sky and explode like thunder. If you heard one, it was never a good sign."

"Say what you will about the alchemists, but they really earn their keep with these." Kallum spread his hands overhead in a bursting motion. "They take on different colors and shapes, some even paint scenes as they burst. Last year, there was a red dragon that flapped its wings across the sky. It truly is a spectacle."

The two prepped the bar for the evening, making various syrups and slicing fruit for cocktails. Rhoren could feel Kallum's lingering gaze as he quartered the limes with trembling hands.

He knew he looked rough. His hands had been shaking too much to pull his hair back in a neat tail, so wispy strands fluttered about his ears. Even as he cut the limes, the fruit vibrated beneath his touch. To his credit, Rhoren managed to slice them without losing a finger.

By twilight, the bar was nearly two-thirds full. Professor Lostwick and some other admin from the university claimed a table at the back where they discussed the book he'd been reading. When Rhoren delivered their drinks, the group assured him that this would be the new location for their monthly book club.

Rhoren thanked them graciously, grateful for more regulars.

James hurried around the room, clearing glasses and silverware. The food cart for the evening served soup in bread bowls, which made for fewer dishes but more cleanup as crumbs scattered across the tables. The boy lurked around the room like a hungry dog searching for scraps, towel in hand to clean tables as quickly as he could.

"Still waiting on him to slow down?" Rhoren asked Kallum when he returned to the bar.

Kallum smirked. "I'm more worried about him taking my job with that work ethic."

The door opened, and a magenta-haired gnome entered. Ametrine's hair sprouted from her head like a flame and she waved at Rhoren animatedly.

His stomach tightened as he waved back at Ametrine. Today was not the day he wanted to deal with the curious gnome.

Rhoren forced a smile. "Welcome!"

She took a seat at the bar. "Since it's after work hours, I decided to spruce up for once." She extended an arm, showcasing her evening attire. Her goggles were replaced with a bedazzled headband that glittered in the candle-light, and instead of the singed work robe she'd worn upon her last visit, she sported a turquoise robe and a cream-colored cloak that fell to her elbows. "I trust the chiller is working well for you."

"Cold as ice." Kallum strained a cocktail into its glass.

"You look nice." Rhoren passed her a menu. "What can we get for you?"

She smiled as she looked it over for a moment. "The Wolfwater Sprite sounds delicious."

He placed the shaker on the bar. "Coming right up."

When Kallum left to deliver a drink, Ametrine leaned forward excitedly. "I still can't believe it. A blood mage in Eastborne and running a tavern. I have so many questions."

Rhoren held a finger to his lips, leaning across the bar. "Look…" He kept his voice low. "Now's not the best time, but I always work alone on Ydden. Come by then and I'll answer any questions you have."

She clapped her hands together, biting her lip as she grinned. "Most excellent! I can't wait."

After Rhoren finished crafting her Wolfwater Sprite, she took the drink and sat around the fire, making conversation with a couple sitting on the couch.

Rhoren shook his head, wondering why people enjoyed gossip so much.

"Someone thinks you're cute." Kallum waggled his brows.

Rhoren laughed. "You don't know the half of it."

Before they knew it, the shift was over and the last of the customers were on their way home.

As Kallum polished bottles and placed them back on the shelves, his face was suddenly serious. "Are you sure you're okay? You've definitely been out of sorts today."

Rhoren stood silent, his gaze settling on the tapestry of the Northern Guard on the far wall. It would be so easy to tell everything to Kallum right now, to reveal his true identity and lay it all out in the open. But what if Kallum hated him for it? Hated him for the things he could never change. The words from their picnic still haunted him. *I have to imagine there's something unsettling about being near someone who could stop your heart from beating just by looking at you.*

He wanted nothing more than to spill his secrets then and there, but the consequences held him back. Without Kallum by his side, he wasn't sure he could run Cursed Cocktails on his own.

But that didn't mean he had to hide everything.

Rhoren set his towel on the bar. "There's something I need to show you."

He led Kallum over to the stairwell and dropped to a knee. A confused expression painted the man's face. When Rhoren pressed a shaky hand against the baseboard and a piece of the wall opened, Kallum's eyes were as wide as saucers.

"By the gods... What is this?" Kallum furrowed his brow as he peeked through the doorway.

Jinx passed between their legs and disappeared into the catacombs.

Rhoren took the lamp from the bar and entered the stairwell. "Last night, I woke up and couldn't find Jinx. I searched everywhere. For a moment I even thought he'd jumped from the balcony into the street." He paused, wondering how to tell the next part without revealing his blood sense. "It turns out there's a way to open this hidden door from both sides. Beneath the stairs inside the bar, and the lever right here." He pointed to the lever inside the hidden stairwell. "Jinx somehow found his way inside."

"What a mischievous little devil." Kallum shook his head in disbelief. "And where does it go exactly?"

"Follow me." Rhoren led him down the stairs. "It connects to the catacombs that run underneath the city."

Kallum stood there with his mouth agape. "I knew that there were hidden tunnels underneath the city, but I had no idea they were still accessible."

"This isn't even the craziest part." He led them down the tunnel, searching the darkness for a hint of blue. When he saw it, he covered the lamp.

"What's going on?" Kallum's voice was higher-pitched than normal.

"Just wait," Rhoren whispered.

The catacombs were dark, save for the sliver of light that spilled down the stairwell where they had entered. Further up the tunnel, what looked like three blue flames swayed in the darkness. Kallum's gasp let Rhoren know that the man saw it, too. Two bright blue eyes approached cautiously until Rhoren crouched and the spirit fox moved closer, sniffing the elf's hands for treats.

"I think she's the one who's been scaring off the other shop owners." He uncovered the lamp, revealing the spirit fox in her entirety, Jinx by her side.

"Wow." Kallum crouched next to Rhoren. "She's beautiful."

"Yeah, I found Jinx curled up with her when I came down."

"This is, I mean, a spirit fox. Just… wow." He held out a hand, and she sniffed at his fingers while Jinx rubbed against the outside of Kallum's leg.

Rhoren smiled. "Crazy, right?"

"Crazy doesn't begin to do it justice. A secret entrance

into an underground labyrinth was crazy enough, but this. I don't even have words. She just lives down here?"

Rhoren shrugged. "I guess so. Hewelet said that they are supposed to watch over the dead. The man in the alchemist colony called her a guardian. Maybe she's drawn to the energy of the place."

"So strange." Kallum looked around. "It has to be lonely for her."

Rhoren found himself laughing unexpectedly.

Kallum gave him a questioning look. "What's so funny?"

Rhoren wiped a tear from his eye. "Maybe it's the lack of sleep, but of all the things I expected you to say, 'she's lonely' wasn't even on the list."

"The unexpected is what gives life its flavor." He stood up, taking Rhoren by the elbow as he did so. "Let's head back and see if we can find this girl some food."

Back at the bar, Kallum gathered some bread and cheese, along with the bowl of soup he'd been planning to save for after his shift, and placed them at the bottom of the stairs. He stroked the spirit fox's fur as she devoured the meal while keeping Jinx from stealing her food with his other hand.

"Come back tomorrow and I'll have something better. You won't go starving on my watch." Kallum scratched underneath her ears before lifting Jinx by the midsection and tossing the cat over his shoulder. Once back inside the tavern, he turned to Rhoren. "I'll finish up down here. You should get some sleep."

"Are you sure?" Rhoren still felt the effects of the previous night, but the last thing he wanted was to burden Kallum.

"I'd love to find out what else is down in the catacombs, but there will be time for that later. We need you at full strength." Kallum winked. "It's going to be a busy week."

"I appreciate it." Rhoren bowed slightly before heading up the stairs.

"And, Rhor, one more thing." He waited for Rhoren to turn around before continuing. "I know you didn't have to show me any of this, but I'm glad you did."

Rhoren smiled and disappeared up the stairs.

Sleep fought for his mind as soon as he lay in bed but before relinquishing his grip on reality, he savored the thought that sharing his secrets with Kallum might not be the worst thing in the world.

29. STORMBRINGER

True to Kallum's word, the streets were packed as people journeyed from the surrounding countryside to attend one of the biggest celebrations in Nelderland. Rhoren had already turned away a dozen customers because they weren't scheduled to open for another hour.

The door opened once again and chatter from the streets spilled inside, followed by Kallum, who quickly shut the door behind him.

He grinned mischievously as he leaned against the closed door with something tucked behind his back. "It's going to be a crazy night."

Rhoren placed the freshly-cut limes into a container. "What has you looking so wicked?"

Kallum revealed a bottle from behind his back with a flourish. "I've got an idea for a special cocktail for the festival."

He held the bottle with pride. It had a wide base and a small handle around the neck, and it was filled with a liquid so dark it looked like tar. A ship with a tentacle wrapping around the hull was etched into the front of the bottle.

Rhoren stopped his prep work to get a closer look. "What in the hells is that?"

"Black rhum." He smirked impishly. "All the way from Barrowsturm."

"Do you drink it or burn it?" Rhoren raised a brow.

Kallum laughed. "Get behind the bar and I'll show you."

Rhoren grinned at Kallum's excitement. No matter how stressful or busy they got, Kallum's love for crafting drinks never faded. It often reminded him of his father's notes and why he'd started this venture to begin with.

"I'll be right over. First, I have a delivery for our new friend." Kallum pulled a container from his satchel and untied the twine. The smell of raw fish carried across the bar.

Jinx jumped on the table, sniffing at the container and pawing at Kallum's arm.

"Not for you." Kallum wagged his finger at the cat.

He activated the mechanism to the hidden entrance with his foot and set the container at the bottom of the stairs before shutting the door with a thud.

"Now where were we?" Kallum asked as he returned to the bar.

Rhoren held up the bottle of viscous black alcohol. "You were about to convince me this goes in a cocktail."

"Have I ever steered you wrong?"

Rhoren smiled. "Alright, alright. Show me what we've got."

Kallum cracked his knuckles and grabbed two glasses from the rack, placing them on the bar. "The first thing we're going to need is ice. Would you like to do the honors?"

Rhoren removed the block of ice from the chiller, chipping away enough to fill both glasses.

"Excellent. Now we'll add some lime juice." Kallum poured a splash of freshly-squeezed lime juice, and Rhoren followed suit. "Next, we'll fill the glass most of the way with ginger beer, like so." He poured a generous amount of ginger beer into the glass.

Rhoren mirrored Kallum's every step, stirring the two elements together with a spoon. "Seems pretty similar to the Nelderland Mule."

"It's not that far off, but the next step is what really sets them apart. We're going to need a spoon for this." He took the spoon and flipped it over, balancing it over the glass. "You're going to want to turn the spoon upside-down, then you'll take the rhum and slowly pour it over the back of the spoon, forming a layer on top of the ginger beer."

Rhoren watched as the black rhum dripped from the spoon's edges, settling on top of the ginger beer. The bottom of the drink had a nice amber color, but the top was dark like a storm cloud.

Kallum finished the drink with a lime wheel garnish and gestured toward his creation. "I call it the Storm-bringer. What do you think?"

"It looks amazing." Rhoren sipped the cocktail. The first drink was boozy and sweet from the black rhum settling on top. The second sip invited the spice from the ginger beer to mix with a hint of tartness and the sweetness of the rhum. "And tastes even better. I love the way each sip offers a new experience as the flavors mix. And with a name like Stormbringer, it's sure to be a hit."

"Good. Now, make your own." Kallum took the drink from Rhoren with a smirk. "This one's mine."

Once the prep work was finished, they opened for business early. The bar filled quickly with people looking for a place to rest for a moment. Through the window, a sea of people flowed past dressed in silver and blue—the traditional colors of the Storm Festival. They looked like a raging river as they moved up and down the street.

Music poured through the open door, and spirits were high all around. By the end of the first hour, they had gone through the entire bottle of black rhum.

"We can scratch that off the menu." Kallum turned the bottle upside-down, draining every last drop over the spoon. "I guess I'll need to order more for tomorrow."

Rhoren walked over to the window, peering into the street. "I don't think our food cart is making it up tonight."

Kallum shrugged. "There's more than enough street vendors to make up for it. Hopefully, James can find a way through all the chaos. I doubt he's ever ventured this high during the festival before."

Rhoren watched as a team of dancers carried a dragon puppet the size of a small boat through the crowd. The dragon was constructed of wood and cloth and was carried high above the crowd suspended on poles. Its silver scales shimmered in the sunlight, and the dancers maneuvered the puppet so that it appeared to be flying through the streets. Each pole controlled a different part of the dragon, and it even had a working jaw that snapped open and closed. People pointed as it flew by, entranced by the wondrous performance.

As it was passing out of sight, James burst through the

crowd, dodging bodies like a nimble-footed rogue as they trampled by.

"Sorry I'm late!" he gasped.

"I'm surprised you made it at all. Sit down and catch your breath for a minute." Rhoren squeezed James's shoulder before returning to the bar. "What's the deal with the dragons?" he asked Kallum.

The man finished garnishing a Nelderland Mule for a burly dwarf at the end of the bar. "You'll see them all over this week. The dragon is supposed to bring in prosperity and a bountiful crop. There's usually a kraken some-where, too—to draw the rain."

"I've never seen anything like it. I can see why everyone enjoys it, though." He felt a childlike wonder himself at all the things he'd missed from his own childhood.

"I imagine you didn't get a lot of parades in the Guard. You should take a moment to enjoy it."

Just as Rhoren was about to take a break, a young man entered the bar surrounded by a gaggle of women. When they parted, a familiar face stepped to the front.

"…the best drinks in Eastborne, I promise." Jesper led them over to the bar. He carried a lute strapped to his back and swayed slightly with each step. "You're even busier than before. I knew this place would be a hit!"

"Someone's enjoying the festivities." Rhoren grinned.

"Full streets means I get the week off. I can finally spend some of this coin I work so hard for. Isn't that right, ladies?"

They all chirped their affirmation.

"So, what'll it be?" asked Kallum.

Jesper counted the number of women in his party.

Then he counted the number of drinks on the menu. "There's six drinks and there's six of us. That seems like a sign to me. One of each!"

A table cleared out as its occupants returned to the festival, so Jesper and his troupe took their place.

"Ah, to be young and spry." The dwarf at the bar tilted his mug in their direction as they sat. "I remember the days when the lasses flocked to me after a long day in the mines."

The man sitting next to him rolled his eyes. "The only thing flocking to you were the flies."

The day carried on, but the atmosphere never faded. Customers came and went, and by the time night had overtaken the city, Jesper had drunk enough to be persuaded to take the stage by his group. He swayed in peaceful bliss as he strummed his lute at the back of the bar.

Kallum leaned toward Rhoren and whispered, "Have you ever heard him sing?"

"How bad could he be?" Rhoren had listened to drunken soldiers carrying tunes for most of his life. Some sang with all the grace of a dying animal. In the north, they took what entertainment they could.

For a long while, Jesper picked at the lute. With eyes closed, he played a soothing melody that entwined with the chatter. When he finally sang, a silence fell over the room.

"When I was young and worked the land,
    And dreamed to soon become a man,
    I came upon a maiden fair,

With ivory skin and auburn hair.

She gazed at me with wanton eyes
And stirred a passion deep inside.
She found me as I forked the hay
And soon within the straw we lay.

On that day, I became a man,
Master over luscious lands.
Little did I know my strife,
For I'd brought to bed the farmer's wife.

I've heard it said so many times,
That women age like dwarven wines.
I can attest from my small part,
I drank my fill and quenched my thirst."

Jesper continued to play, and whispers snaked through the bar, commenting on his singing.

"By the gods, he has the voice of a siren." Kallum was visibly shocked. "How is he not performing seven nights a week? Hells, Timofey would pay him good money to sing at the Seaside Inn."

Rhoren grinned. "I guess now we know why he has so many admirers."

"With a voice like that, he could have the entire city eating out of his hand."

The song continued, further detailing his exploits with

the ladies of various towns and villages. The entire bar was engrossed in his performance, and people had even filtered through the doorway to listen.

When he finished, Jesper took a bow to great applause and walked over to the bar. He took a deep breath. "I'm going to need a drink."

"It's on the house." Rhoren winked. "How did you never tell us you had such a lovely voice?"

"Lovely?" Jesper blushed. "I only sing when I've had a drink too many but not one too much."

Rhoren laughed. "Well, you can sing here anytime."

After another drink, Jesper played again. And again. To the point that no one was leaving the bar and it was standing room only. James weaseled his way through the crowd, cleaning tables and bussing glassware. Jinx was lost somewhere among the chaos, occasionally making a visit behind the bar for a head-scratch or two.

Eventually, Jesper put the lute away—to the dismay of his newfound fans—and people began to trickle out. It was late before the bar finally emptied and the streets returned to a semblance of normality. Rhoren asked James to sweep the floors and wipe the tables, then he paid the boy and sent him on his way.

"This was quite a night." Rhoren organized the bar, wiping things down and storing them in their proper place.

"I'd say." Kallum stood at the other end of the bar, polishing glassware. "I still can't believe a farm-boy can sing like that."

"In my experience, people are full of surprises. You know—"

The glass Kallum was polishing broke, and the

resounding crack held all the anticipation of crunching ice on a frozen lake. There was a moment of stillness, where Kallum looked down in disbelief at the crimson ribbon on his hand, followed by a groan as he grimaced. He winced as bright red blood poured down his arm, streaking his shirt and speckling the floor.

Kallum raised his arm, revealing a large gash along his palm where blood flowed freely. It dripped from his elbow like rain on a clay roof. His face was stark white as he leaned against the wall.

Rhoren rushed to his side, pressing a towel against the wound.

"Easy there. It's just a cut," he said calmly. "Let's put some pressure on it to slow the bleeding." After making sure Kallum wasn't going to pass out, he guided the man's free hand to the towel. "Hold this firm. I'll get my kit from upstairs."

From his time in the wilderness, Rhoren had learned to always travel with a kit for treating wounds. He never knew what awaited on those dangerous missions, and being prepared was the difference between life and death for him and his men.

Rhoren moved with purpose as he pulled the kit from underneath the bed. When he returned, Jinx stood next to Kallum as he sat with his back to the wall, licking the man's hand.

"I'll take it from here, Jinx."

Jinx meowed before flopping onto his side.

"I don't know what happened." Kallum's voice weak, scared. He stared down at his hand as if it was a foreign object.

Rhoren knelt beside him. He doubted the man had

ever seen this much blood in his life. He took Kallum's hand and pulled back the crimson bar towel. The gash was deep, and blood pooled immediately. He pressed the towel to the wound again and looked Kallum in the eyes. The man was ghastly white.

He gave his best reassuring smile. "Don't worry. I'll get you fixed up soon enough."

The good news was that glass cut cleanly. He'd brought men back from worse, from wounds born of teeth and claws that weren't so forgiving. He could stop the flow of blood with his magic if needed, but he would still have to stitch the wound. Considering his own sensitivity to calling on his magic nowadays, it would be safer for all parties to do this the old-fashioned way.

Rhoren squeezed Kallum's fingers gently. He'd learned long ago that talking to someone helped take their mind off whatever was happening. "You're going to be fine. First, I need to stop the bleeding. I'm going to sprinkle some Devil's Nettle in the wound. It'll sting, but it will allow me to clean you up."

Kallum nodded.

Rhoren took a pouch from his kit and unwrapped the leather tie. An earthy smell immediately filled the area. After dabbing the wound once more with the towel, he sprinkled the powdered plant into the cut. Kallum grimaced and his arm tensed, but he held back his screams.

"We're almost there, Kal." He caressed Kallum's face with the back of his knuckles, and their eyes locked. "I'm going to disinfect the wound to make sure you don't get an infection."

Rhoren grabbed a bottle of watka and removed the

stopper with his mouth. "Here, take a drink. It'll help with the pain."

Kallum took the bottle with his free hand and turned it up. Rhoren pointed to the ceiling, and when Kallum looked up, he doused the wound with alcohol, revealing the pink flesh underneath the blood. Kallum cursed and pushed his back against the wall. The cut was deep but clean and good for healing. Inside the wound, a sliver of glass gleamed.

Using a pair of tweezers, Rhoren removed the glass shard. "The worst is over. I'm going to stitch you up now."

Kallum closed his eyes, taking heavy breaths. With each stitch, his face contorted with pain. Rhoren continued to talk, and soon, the wound was closed.

Rhoren lifted Kallum's hand, examining the stitches. "It should heal fine on its own, but we can get you to a cleric to be safe."

Kallum reached for the watka, but Rhoren moved it away.

"I know it helps with the pain, but too much and you'll bleed through your stitches."

Kallum looked at his wound. "In all my years bartending, I've never had an accident like this. I don't know what I would have done without you."

Rhoren patted him on the shoulder. "It looked worse than it was. Even if you passed out, you'd be fine. You'd be sore and have a headache worse than death from the blood loss, but you'd live."

"Thank you." Kallum's gaze was intense.

Rhoren looked away. "It was nothing."

"It was everything. I can see why you were a good

soldier. You rushed to my aid without hesitation. I don't know what my life would be without you in it."

Rhoren grinned. "You'd probably still be working at the Seaside Inn with two good hands."

"Don't do that." There was an edge to his words. "I mean it, Rhoren. My life is better because you are in it."

Rhoren's face fell as the sincerity of the words cut him like a knife. Would Kallum still feel that way if he knew the truth?

Kallum must have noticed his reaction because he took Rhoren's hand in his uninjured one. "What?"

Rhoren sat there staring at the wall. If Kallum truly felt the way he said, then it wouldn't matter that Rhoren was a blood mage.

He took a deep breath, feeling the warmth of Kallum's hand in his own trembling fingers. "There's something I need to tell you." He swallowed, surprised at the shakiness of his voice. "I haven't been completely honest with you." He released Kallum's hand. "It's true that I served in the Northern Guard but not as a soldier."

Kallum frowned, some of the color already returning to his face. "What then?"

Rhoren's throat tightened, but he forced the words out. "I was—I *am* a blood mage."

Kallum's lips curled at the edge. When it was clear that Rhoren wasn't joking, his eyes widened. "A blood mage? You? But how?"

Rhoren didn't meet the man's eyes, instead watching his own hands. "Blood magic takes a toll on the body. Over the years, each time I called on it, it left me more scarred. Every time took longer for the effects to subside. When I finally earned my retirement, a cleric suggested that I move south to see if the climate might help with the pain."

"Has it?"

The question caught Rhoren by surprise. He'd expected revulsion, maybe even fear, but curiosity over his well-being? It hadn't even crossed his mind.

"Yes, but I used my power the other day when I couldn't find Jinx. The effects are worse than ever when I call upon it now."

"That explains why you were out of sorts." Kallum took Rhoren's hand again. "I knew there was something you weren't telling me."

Rhoren frowned. He tried to let go of Kallum's hand, but the man held firm. None of this was going as he'd expected, and a maelstrom of emotions swirled inside of him.

"What's wrong?" Kallum asked.

"You're not angry?" He glanced at Kallum's face—a face painted with concern.

"Angry? Why would I be angry?" His tone was soft, comforting. "I understand why you would want to keep that part of yourself secret."

"But what you said about blood mages that day at our picnic. I don't know, I just... I thought you would hate what I am."

Kallum placed a hand on Rhoren's chin, forcing the umbral elf to meet his eyes. "Whatever I said that day was born out of ignorance. You could tell me you're a demon, for all I care. It doesn't matter. Whatever you are, underneath it all, you are a good person, Rhoren. And that is all that matters."

Rhoren's cheeks flared with heat, and his vision

blurred at the edges. How had he ever doubted Kallum's character?

Kallum stood, groaning as he did so. He staggered for a moment, then stretched out his arms. "You look like you need a hug."

When they embraced, tension poured from Rhoren's body. A lifetime of weight left his shoulders as he held Kallum tight. For the first time since that terrible night long ago, Rhoren felt safe. He squeezed a little tighter, never wanting to let go.

30. MENDING

Rhoren and Kallum agreed that they would find a cleric the next morning. While the wound would heal fine on its own, it would still be tender for a few days and probably hinder Kallum from the normal legerity with which he crafted drinks. A cleric could speed the healing along so that he could still tend bar without issue.

With the Storm Festival in full swing, they would need everyone working at full strength.

Kallum was still a bit shaken, so Rhoren insisted he stay the night, letting the man use his bed while he slept on the couch downstairs. Jinx stayed with Kallum, giving Rhoren all the solace he needed to process his thoughts.

The secret he'd been hiding since arriving in Eastborne had been revealed, and it had gone better than he could have hoped. Kallum would certainly have more questions, but that didn't matter. Rhoren would answer every one.

In the end, all that mattered was that Kallum had accepted Rhoren for who he was.

Rhoren kept that in his forethoughts as he drifted off to the most peaceful sleep he'd had in ages.

He slept so soundly that he didn't wake when the secret door opened. When a cold, wet nose pressed against his dangling arm, he nearly screamed from the shock.

The spirit fox tilted its head, watching Rhoren cycle through various states of alarm before chuckling to himself.

The sun was just starting to breach through the windows.

"Good morning to you, too." Rhoren extended a hand, letting the fox sniff his fingers. "I guess I should get used to you wandering around now that the fox is out of the catacombs, as they say." She stepped closer, and Rhoren scratched behind her ears, causing the three tails to swish in unison. "Just stay hidden during working hours."

"Who are you talking to?" Kallum peeked his head around the stairwell. His beard and hair were disheveled from sleep, but color had returned to his cheeks. He looked much better than he had the night before.

There was a patter of feet as Jinx ran down the stairs, pouncing on the spirit fox with a playful tackle. The two thrashed about the barroom floor meowing and growling with pleasure.

"My new roommate, I guess." Rhoren grinned. "Ready to get you fixed up?"

Kallum held up his hand. "I'm a little stiff, but it's not as bad as I thought. My head is killing me, though."

Rhoren went to the bar, chipping some ice into a glass and filling it with soda water and a squeeze of lime. "This should help."

Soon after, they found themselves walking through the streets toward the nearest temple. Children hurried about, filling carts with litter from the day before. Kallum explained that the children were hired by the council to clean the streets every year for the festival. It put coin in the pockets of many families across the river and kept the streets presentable during a time when they were over-crowded.

As they passed an alleyway, they spotted several men passed out from the night before. Rhoren paused, watching the men as they grumbled in their drunkenness.

Kallum shook his head as he laughed. "There are those who enjoy the festival, and then there are those who are consumed by it."

The temple was nearly identical in its design to those in the north. The only difference was the gods depicted inside. There were many gods across Aedrea, and while all were worshipped to some degree, certain ones held prominence in different areas.

This particular temple featured a statue of Ahteus, the God of Fortune. The god was broad-shouldered and bald, with a staff in one hand and a sword in the other. A calf curled at his feet to one side and a chest filled with trea-sures flanked the other. The wall behind the statue had a stained-glass starburst, and the morning light set the statue ablaze in a rainbow of color.

A hooded cleric knelt at the pulpit, praying.

Rhoren cleared his throat. "Excuse me, we need some help."

"Blessed fortune to you." The cleric turned around, revealing the gnome's forest green hair framed by the baggy hood of the robe. "We don't often get many visitors this—"

The cleric stopped in his tracks when he noticed the emblem on Rhoren's cloak. Even though his cloak from the Guard was too warm for the climate, he'd purposely chosen it for this occasion.

"Sir." The gnome bowed slightly. "Thank you for your —" He looked to Kallum and then back to Rhoren. "—service."

"It's okay." Rhoren smiled. "He knows."

"Very well." The cleric nodded. "How may I be of service, Bloodbane?"

Rhoren stirred at the mention of his moniker.

"Bloodbane?" Kallum's eyes widened. "Even I've heard that name. You mean to tell me that that is you?"

"Yes, that's me." Rhoren's cheeks flushed. "Can we deal with the matter at hand first?"

"Bloodbane," Kallum whispered to himself in awe. "I'm running a bar with the one called Bloodbane."

Rhoren ignored Kallum's rambling, returning his attention to the cleric. "My friend here had an accident last night. He has a nasty cut along his palm, and while I was able to stitch it up, he's not in the best shape for bartending. I was hoping you could help speed the healing along."

"I've heard about your bar. Cursed Cocktails, is it?" The cleric nodded approvingly. "I thought the name was quite clever myself. I've heard great things, but we were given explicit instructions by the Order of Clerics to stay away in order to protect your anonymity."

"I appreciate it. Though, I feel my days of obscurity are

nearing an end." Ametrine's scheduled visit crossed his mind briefly.

"You have earned your privacy if you choose it. The realm is forever in your debt." The gnome's face was solemn. "Let me see the wound, if you please."

The cleric mumbled to himself as he inspected the cut on Kallum's hand, commenting on the quality of Rhoren's stitchwork and how clean the wound was.

When he'd seen enough, he looked up. "Shouldn't take more than an hour to mend."

A mending was rather simple as far as restorative abilities went, and almost any cleric across the realm could perform one on minor wounds. Not all clerics were created equal, however, so the Order of Clerics dispensed their members where they were needed most.

There were still many ailments that clerics couldn't heal—certain poisons, curses, mana drain, and in Rhoren's case, the ravages of blood magic.

The three of them sat on a pew while the cleric performed the mending. The gnome prayed to his deity, placing both hands around Kallum's. As the words poured from his mouth, a golden glow emanated from the cleric's palms, enveloping Kallum's hand in ethereal energy.

"It's warm. Like a hot bath." Kallum wore a surprised expression. "You know, in all my years, this is actually the first time I've ever needed a cleric." He looked at Rhoren. "What about you?"

Rhoren laughed. "More times than I can count."

The cleric kept his attention focused on the mending as Rhoren and Kallum talked.

"So, did you actually fight them? The behemoths." Kallum waited expectantly.

"I did. On more occasions than I care to remember." Rhoren paid careful attention to Kallum's expressions.

Kallum's shoulders stiffened. "I bet it was terrifying."

Rhoren nodded. "At first, it was. I still remember the first time I traveled into the wilderness. We had twenty guardsmen with us. I was young, still in training, so Ailen took the lead. She was as talented and powerful as any blood mage I've ever known, and one of the few who never seemed to tire of the hunt. When I heard the behemoth roar, it froze me in my tracks. Even now, I can recall the feeling. I wondered how I could ever hope to stop something like that."

Kallum slid forward in the pew slightly, though not enough to affect the cleric's work. "What happened?"

"Ailen brought the behemoth down from a hundred yards away. One moment the monstrous creature was rushing toward us, its daunting roar reverberating in my chest. The next, it collapsed into the snow. Ailen had more respect than any blood mage I've known because she never put her men in harm's way. But if she had needed them, a thousand men would have died trying to help her."

"She sounds like an amazing woman. Was your father a blood mage, too?"

Rhoren's features darkened as he traveled back to that night in his mind. The night his world fell apart and he discovered what he truly was. If his father had been a blood mage, everything would have been different.

"No," Rhoren whispered. "He wasn't."

Kallum continued to delve into Rhoren's life in the Guard. The answers weren't always warm and fuzzy, but for Rhoren's part, he was happy to answer, glad to finally have nothing holding him back from being his truest self.

When the mending was finished, Kallum flexed his hand, curling each finger in turn. "Gods be good, it's like it never happened."

Rhoren extended his hand to the gnome. "Thank you..." He paused, realizing he didn't know the cleric's name.

"Odric, sir."

"Thank you, Odric. Stop by Cursed Cocktails anytime you feel inclined."

The gnome smiled. "I just might do that."

"You better." Kallum wrapped his arm around the cleric. "Your drinks are on me."

A trumpet blared from outside the temple, and through the open door, a troupe of musicians could be seen marching up the street.

Rhoren stood, removing his cloak and draping it over his arm. "I think that's our cue to go. If we're even half as busy as last night, we need to start preparing now, starting with getting as much black rhum as we can carry."

31. SURPRISES

The Storm Festival brought a whirlwind of excitement, each day busier than the one before. Talk of the Northern Guard and blood magic fell to the wayside, replaced by drink orders and rowdy choruses. Jesper lived in a perpetual state of celebration, returning night after night to the delight of the patrons. Even a certain cleric made an appearance to take Kallum up on his offer.

Cursed Cocktails found success during the madness of the festival, and the days began to blur together. By the final night, there wasn't a bottle of black rhum to be found in Eastborne.

"It's time!" someone shouted from the porch. "The firelights are about to start!"

The barroom cleared as everyone hurried out into the crowded street.

"I can't see!" James complained as he bounced on his tiptoes, trying to look over the shoulders of those around him.

"Don't worry." Kallum tried to assure him. "The show

happens in the sky, but if it makes you feel better, you can climb on my shoulders."

Kallum knelt, and the boy crawled up his back, draping a leg over each shoulder.

"Look, I'm a giant!" James beamed as he towered over the crowd.

Rhoren was busy laughing at the pair when the first firelight streamed across the sky. A trail of blue shot up from the docks like a shooting star, passing in front of the moon. A moment later, there was a thunderous clap and a burst of blue exploded across the sky.

The crowd gasped in unison, and no sooner had the first firelight faded before two more crisscrossed overhead. Red and yellow sparkled against the night to the delight of the city.

Oohs and ahhs passed through the crowded streets as if the entire city was under the same spell. Firelights fizzled and exploded. Some swirled in elaborate patterns or painted pictures in the sky, their lights lingering long after the original burst.

The final display ignited the night with a barrage that reflected on the sea. A sparkling ship sailed through the sky, waves rippling around it. As the waves dissipated, a kraken formed beneath the ship, and long tentacles wrapped around the hull. A final explosion burst as the hull cracked, and the firelights faded as the kraken pulled the ship into its mouth.

Celebration broke out across Eastborne as people clapped and music resumed in the streets. Rhoren and Kallum returned to the bar, crafting drinks until the wee hours of the morning.

Over the next week, the city gradually returned to its normal state. Even though people moved about with their midday business, the streets looked empty by comparison. Rhoren was looking forward to a peaceful evening tending bar by himself. After the past two weeks, he felt he could handle even a normal night solo. The sheer volume of drinks they'd crafted during the festival had improved his speed dramatically.

There was usually a lull before the first customers arrived, but when he opened the door, a magenta-haired gnome looked up at him with excitement. Ametrine must have come straight from the Runecrafter's Guild, because she still wore her goggles and singed robe.

"How long have you been standing there?" Rhoren stepped aside, gesturing for her to enter.

Ametrine shrugged. "Not long. I just left work, but I didn't want to be rude." She walked past Rhoren, taking a seat at the bar. "Did you enjoy the festival? I don't know if I've ever seen the city this full."

"I did. I've never seen anything quite like it." Rhoren smiled as he passed her a menu. In the chaos of the festival, he'd forgotten all about the invitation for the peppy gnome. "What can I get for you?"

She tapped her chin as she looked over the piece of parchment. "It says here you have wine. Anything from Revelia?"

"We have a few things. Kallum worked hard to make sure we have an extensive wine list from across the realm." He took a wine menu from the shelf and placed it on the bar. "Let's see. We have a golden wine from Cogwall and an icewine from Aethervale."

"I love icewine!" She clapped her hands together. "A glass of that, please. With a little ice, if you have it."

"You know we do." He took a block of ice from the chiller and searched the wine rack.

He filled a glass with ice, and it crackled as he poured the wine over it.

Ametrine sniffed the wine before taking a long sip. Her eyes fluttered and she sighed. "It's been years since I've been home, but drinking this, it takes me right back. Funny how that works, isn't it? A certain smell or taste can transport you back to somewhere you haven't been in years."

Rhoren knew the feeling all too well. The aroma of his mother's fireweed tea was seared into his memory. The herb was rare outside of Sanguine, but on the rare times he encountered it, the minty citrus smell always took him back to that night.

He leaned against the bar. It was best to satiate the gnome's curiosity and get this over with. "You said you have questions?"

Ametrine set her glass down and slid forward on the stool. "So many questions! I've always found blood magic fascinating. It's unlike any other type of magic, you know, wondrous and terrifying in its capabilities. And, I'm sure you know—what am I saying? Of course you do—blood mages are hard to find outside of the Northern Guard. And, well, I was just hoping I could pick your brain and maybe understand it a little bit better. I mean, I've read about it, but you know, nothing is better than a primary source."

She took a deep breath, followed by another drink of wine. Her periwinkle eyes sparkled as she waited for his answer. Rhoren wasn't sure he'd ever seen anyone speak so much without taking a breath.

"What is it you want to know?" Rhoren held up a finger as Ametrine was about to speak. "But first, there are some rules. I appreciate your curiosity, but I am not one of your experiments. I will answer three questions for you, with as much depth and detail as I am capable. Yes, I'm a blood mage. It is part of who I am, but it does not define me. So when we're done, I would appreciate it if you would remember that."

She gulped. "Three questions. Got it. May I have some time to think?"

Rhoren laughed. "Take all the time you need."

Ametrine took her wine and meandered around the bar. Jinx followed her, chasing after a stray thread that dangled from her robe.

Soon after, Dingo arrived with his food cart, bemoaning the missed opportunity of not being stationed outside the bar during the festival.

"How about a drink to ease your troubles?" Rhoren pointed to the menu. "I'm sure you were plenty busy down by the docks, right? I could see the crowd in the glow of the firelights."

Dingo scoffed. "You've spoiled me, Rhoren. I was busy, sure, but it's not the same. I'd much rather sell a dozen oysters to someone happy from a drink than half that to someone breaking their back on the docks." He shook his head. "Working too hard makes the man hard, and not in a good way."

A few more patrons soon arrived, and Dingo took to his post out front.

When James showed up, his face was sullen—a far cry from the joyous boy who'd ridden Kallum's shoulders the week before.

Rhoren pulled him aside. "Everything okay?"

James blinked rapidly to hold back the tears. "Father came in this morning."

Rhoren patted the boy on the back. "That sounds like good news. Why so glum?"

"He's leaving again tomorrow." James's brow furrowed, and a mixture of anger and sadness swirled across his face.

"I see." Rhoren wrapped his arm around James. "Your father is a good man, but not even he controls the tides. Why don't you take the night off and spend some quality time with him?"

James looked up at Rhoren. "But Kallum's not here to help you."

"Don't you worry about me." Rhoren ruffled the boy's sandy blonde hair. "Have Dingo send some oysters home with you, and give your father and Cindy my best."

James wrapped his arms around Rhoren, squeezing his midsection with all the strength a young boy could muster.

When Rhoren looked up, Ametrine had returned to the bar. James sprinted out the door, startling Jinx and sending the cat bolting up the stairs.

The gnome grinned at Rhoren. "That was sweet."

"He's a good kid. So, are you ready to ask your first question?" asked Rhoren.

"Ooh, I love a good question." Kallum stepped through

the door holding a bottle of forest-green liquor. "What's the subject?"

Rhoren's eyes widened. "It's your day off. What are you doing here?"

He waved the bottle. "Special delivery this morning. I had this one sent to my place so it could be a surprise. It's a good thing I showed up, too. I ran into James on my way in, and he said you gave him the night off."

"Tomas is on a quick turnaround, so I thought he might appreciate the extra time together."

"Can't argue with that." Kallum shifted his gaze between Rhoren and Ametrine. "So, what are we talking about?"

Ametrine froze, looking to Rhoren for guidance.

Rhoren found more than a small amount of amusement in the gnome's discomfort. "It seems you're not the only one who loves to gossip, Kal. Ametrine's cousin is a cleric, and he let it slip that there was a blood mage in town. She's been pestering me for an interview ever since."

Ametrine's normally rose-pink cheeks were a deep red.

Kallum pulled up a seat next to her, setting the bottle on the bar. "You must introduce me to your cousin."

"You know?" she whispered before turning to Rhoren. "He knows?"

Rhoren laughed. "Yes, he knows."

She slouched forward. "Gods, I thought I had ruined everything."

Kallum grinned. "I only found out recently myself, so I'm equally as intrigued as you are."

"Let's get on with it then." Rhoren tossed the polishing rag over his shoulder. "The less ears around the better."

"Okay." Ametrine sat up straight. "I guess the first thing I'd want to know is how you found out you were a blood mage? I'd imagine it would be a pretty alarming thing to discover if you weren't prepared for it."

Rhoren's ears rang as his mind traveled back in time. The dull chatter of the patrons scattered around the room muffled even more. He knew this question would come eventually. If not from Ametrine, then Kallum. Still, it didn't make it any easier to deal with.

That memory was always with him, but it was like a puzzle with pieces that had been removed. The cold. The smell of fireweed tea. His father's terror-stricken face as he led Rhoren and his mother across the village. A roar that sent ice through his veins. And then blackness.

He knew what happened next—there was no way he could ever forget—but it was like his mind had hidden it away from him. The next thing he could picture was himself, alone, muffled whispers all around him, and the dead eyes of the behemoth as it sprawled across the snow.

Rhoren took a deep breath. The ringing faded, and the soft voices of the table nearby crashed like an avalanche. He released his breath and focused on the two before him. Even though they hadn't moved, there was an expectation in their stillness.

"I was a young boy, only six years old, when the behemoth attacked our town. We heard its devastation long before we saw it. The crack of wood splintering as it tore through buildings. Distant screams of umbral elves as it ripped them apart. It was the dead of winter, and we had nowhere to go, but as the sounds grew closer, my father made a choice." He paused. In that moment, Rhoren's face could have been etched in stone. "We took off running. I don't know where he was leading us, but the monster… Somehow, it found us. My father tried to fight it off. I'll never forget the silhouette of his body standing over me as he faced it down. It didn't matter, though. The monster killed him without a thought. My mother, too. And in that moment, I only wanted the thing to die. And then it did."

Rhoren fixed his gaze on the bar. He'd never talked to anyone about what had happened. There were enough witnesses that he hadn't needed to, and once he joined the Guard, it was a thing of the past, a catalyst that had brought him there. His focus became training, so he could make sure it never happened to anyone else.

Kallum's hand wrapped around Rhoren's, offering a reassuring squeeze. Rhoren looked up, and there was nothing but compassion in the man's eyes. Silent tears painted Ametrine's cheeks.

"That's awful," she whispered. "I'm sorry. This was a bad idea."

She made a move to get up, but Rhoren stopped her.

"It's okay." He nodded reassuringly. "It's good to remember, to remind people that this is what the Northern Guard fights for. They sacrifice so that things like that don't happen."

She offered a sympathetic smile. "Your father sounds like a brave elf."

"I like to think he was." Rhoren cleared his throat. "What was your next question?"

Whatever it was, nothing would be harder to talk about than the first.

Ametrine waited a moment before asking, taking a

long drink of her icewine. "What does it feel like?"

"Pain," Rhoren answered matter-of-factly. "When it comes to blood magic, everything is pain. There's a reason some call us the Cursed Ones. The price to use our powers drives us mad more than any other magic user. Blood magic is powered from within, and it ravages the body as a result. In the beginning, the body heals. The pain lasts for a moment before the body mends itself. After a while, the effects linger. That's why I found myself in Eastborne, hoping for a little relief from all my body has endured."

Both Ametrine and Kallum wore pained expressions. It was clear by their reactions that not many knew the physical toll that blood magic took on the body, let alone the mental toll that accompanied it.

"That sounds awful." She grimaced. "I've seen what mana drain can do to a mage who pushes too hard, but to have everything you do eat away at your being... It only makes me respect you more."

A group of three men entered, putting a pause to the conversation while Rhoren took their orders. He crafted the drinks in silence.

After delivering the drinks to their table, Rhoren returned his attention to Ametrine. "I believe I still owe you one more answer."

She stared at him for a long moment. "If you had the power to change things, to go back in time and give up your blood magic, would you?"

He'd asked himself the same thing many times. On cold nights when he felt alone in the world, and the only comfort was the words in his father's journal.

Rhoren shook his head. "Never. As much as I have lost,

and as much as I have suffered, I wouldn't change a thing. During my time in the Guard, I stopped countless behemoths from traveling south. There is no telling how many atrocities were prevented because I was there to stop them. There is no way to tell how many boys will grow up under the watchful eyes of their fathers because those monsters were put to rest. My past is what gave me the conviction to press onward even when the burden seemed too heavy to continue. Everything that has happened to me as a result of blood magic I take as a consequence of my powers, not as a punishment for having them."

"I appreciate you taking the time to humor me." Ametrine looked almost ashamed as she sipped the last of her wine. "If I'd known the things you've endured, I would have kept my silly mouth shut."

"There's no need for that." Rhoren winked. "It does me good to remember, and you are welcome here any time."

Ametrine thanked Rhoren for his time and left after settling her tab. Kallum sat in silence at the bar. Rhoren imagined the heavy thoughts that might be on the man's mind.

"Jinx got your tongue?" Rhoren asked.

Kallum offered a half-smile. "Just thinking."

Rhoren rested his elbows on the bar. "What about?"

"How lucky we are. It's easy to lose sight of the world beyond the city streets. It seems so selfish."

"It's not selfish, Kal. That's just life. We all have our struggles, and all we can do is face the ones that stand before us." Rhoren smiled. "Starting with this mysterious bottle you brought in."

Kallum laughed. "You really have a way of putting

things in perspective."

Rhoren placed two glasses on the bar. "There's a lifetime to brood on your circumstances. Why not have a drink first?"

"Alright, fine." Kallum's infectious smile returned. "You're not going to believe what I got my hands on."

Rhoren had observed the bottle when Kallum first set it down, but there was no label or discernible features to help identify its contents.

Kallum searched behind the bar for the space where Rhoren kept his father's journal. When he found it, he flipped through the pages, laying the journal face open on the bar when he found the page he was looking for.

"You didn't?" Rhoren's mouth dropped open. "I checked with every supplier in the city. Most of them had never even heard of the elixir, much less how to find it. How did you manage?"

Kallum stroked his beard while mischief played across his eyes. "Let's just say I have my own secrets."

Rhoren ran his finger over the recipe.

The Final Word

Ingredients:

1 oz Lime Juice
1 oz Cherry Liqueur
1 oz Tiberian Monk's Herbal Elixir (green)
1 oz Dry Jin

He'd wondered if he would ever have a chance to try this particular cocktail. According to his father's notes,

the herbal elixir was produced for its medicinal properties and was extremely hard to come by.

"You're really not going to tell me?" Rhoren raised an
eyebrow.

"And spoil the fun?" Kallum cradled the bottle like a
newborn child. "You mentioned wanting to try this cocktail the first time you ever showed me your father's journal. The elixir was hard to track down, but I called in a
few favors. My family lives in Tiberia, remember? I sent a
letter to my father, and he happened to know someone
who owns a boutique that specializes in rare potions and
tonics."

Rhoren placed his hands together in prayer. "Gods
bless that man."

Kallum held the bottle out to Rhoren. "Want to give it
a try?"

"You never cease to amaze me." Rhoren took the
bottle, feeling the weight of it in his hands. With it, he
could craft the first cocktail his father had ever written in
the journal. "How about after the shift? This is one I'd like
to savor."

"I can't wait."

There was the patter of feet as Jinx rushed down the
stairs, and a moment later the door opened. Helena
limped inside, favoring her right leg. Jinx extended his
front paws, reaching up to the woman's midsection as she
scratched him behind the ears.

"Who's a sweetheart?" she asked him with more
compassion than she had ever spoken to another person.

"You alright, Helena?" Rhoren waved. "You're moving
a little tenderly."

"There's a storm coming in." She frowned. "I can feel it

in my bones."

Rhoren walked to the window and looked out. The sun was fading, and dark clouds brewed on the horizon. "I guess the festival was a success."

She sat down in a chair near the fireplace with a groan, and Jinx curled around her feet. "Be careful what you wish for."

The shift passed by, and even though Rhoren could have handled it on his own, Kallum stayed. After the past two weeks, it was a welcome downtime.

Once the bar cleared out, Rhoren opened his father's notebook and placed it on the bar. "Shall we?"

He opened the journal to the first page and read his father's words, the words that had guided Rhoren down this path since long before he saw the empty storefront that would become Cursed Cocktails.

One day, when these pages are filled and my travels are done, I hope to open my own tavern and share its contents with the world. -Dhorian Balsalor

Rhoren whispered to himself, "While it might not have happened in the way you imagined, we're sharing your work with the world."

"He'd be proud of what you've built." Kallum gripped Rhoren's shoulder. "And I'm proud to be a part of it."

Rhoren flipped the page, revealing the recipe for The Final Word.

Kallum lined the bar with the four ingredients for the cocktail. "It's really a simple recipe at heart. It's what's inside that sets it apart. And I can honestly say that I have no idea what we are in for with this one."

They added lime juice, cherry liqueur, dry jin, and the herbal elixir into a shaker. After filling it with ice, they shook the ingredients together vigorously until a cool sheen coated the outside.

"You don't see this often, but we're going to double strain this one." Kallum handed Rhoren a strainer for the shaker and another fine strainer to go over the glass.

As he poured the contents through both strainers, pulp from the lime juice and small flecks of herbs were filtered out, and a yellowish-green liquid filled the coupe glass, giving the refined glass a toxic appearance that wouldn't be out of place in the alchemist colony.

Kallum used a peeler to make a lime swirl and dropped it in the center of the glass with a flourish. "Now, that is a good-looking drink." He toasted to Rhoren. "Shall we?"

Rhoren clinked his glass against Kallum's and took a sip. It was bright and tart, but with a subtle sweetness that balanced the drink flawlessly.

"It's perfect." He gestured toward a table, and Kallum followed.

As they sat there in silence, enjoying their drinks, Jinx pawed at the hidden entrance. There was a click from within the wall, and a moment later, the door swung open. The spirit fox sniffed at the air as she entered, and Jinx nuzzled against her.

The two animals played together, pouncing on the furniture and chasing one another around the room, while Rhoren and Kallum shared a beautiful silence, neither one daring to break the moment. As his head began to swirl from the drink, Rhoren couldn't help but feel he was right where he belonged.

32. KRAKEN'S DELIGHT

Several days passed before Helena's prediction came true. Rhoren shivered from behind the bar. The weather would still be considered warm by northern standards, but the temperature was noticeably cooler than he was used to in Eastborne. The chill had come in like a crashing wave, dropping dramatically between the tolls of the midday bells.

Helena sat in front of the fireplace, enjoying a glass of wine as Kallum lit the fire for the first time.

"See? These bones don't lie." She wore a smug look as she petted Jinx, and the massive cat purred in her lap. "A storm's coming."

"We know." Kallum narrowed his eyes at the woman. "We could hear your body creaking as you walked in."

Rhoren coughed to conceal his laugh as the old woman's mouth hung open.

Kallum grinned mischievously when he returned to the bar.

"Must you provoke her?" Rhoren narrowed his eyes but couldn't conceal the mirth within.

"It's all good fun." Kallum winked. "She can give as good as she gets."

"It's not her I'm worried about." Rhoren smirked.

The night wore on, and guests flocked to the food cart selling freshly-baked meat pies. Steam plumed from each table as a savory aroma filled the bar.

"You'd think they'd never been cold before." Rhoren shook his head, even though he was feeling the chill himself.

"It's a hard life living in such a paradise. Once or twice a year, we must light a fire or else be forced to put a second blanket on the bed." Kallum rolled his eyes. "But remember that this too shall pass."

Rain began to patter in the streets, and Helena turned to face the bar, pursing her lips in an "I told you so" look. Kallum waved her off, but Rhoren's mind was elsewhere.

"If there is a storm, what happens to all the ships?" he asked.

"If it's a little rain, not much. Anything worse, and they all come to shore." Kallum's brow furrowed. "What's troubling you?"

Rhoren fixed his gaze on the window, where droplets began to cling to the glass. "Tomas is still out at sea, and I've never given much thought to the perils of open water. I was never stationed by a port."

"I'm sure he'll be fine." Kallum gripped Rhoren's shoulder. "He's a seasoned sailor, and it's been years since we've had a bad storm. Even so, if they can't make it to the harbor, they'll beach the ship before they sail into danger."

Kallum's words offered relief to Rhoren's worries, but

he'd been trained to prepare for the worst and expect the unexpected. He flexed his own fingers, which still held the dullest memory of the ache from the last time he'd used his blood magic, and couldn't help but wonder what Helena's bones were telling her.

The next day, the rain fell even harder. Dozens of ships could be seen making for the docks before fog engulfed the harbor. Streams of rain flowed through the streets, and Cursed Cocktails was nearly empty. Helena sat by the fire, and a man who'd come in to escape the rain hunched over a puddle at the nearest table.

Thunder cracked overhead, and the building shuddered in response.

"Kraken's Delight," the man mumbled as he squeezed water from the bottom of his robe.

"What's that?" asked Rhoren.

The man looked up from the task at hand. "That's what the sailors call it when the fog rolls in during a thunderstorm—Kraken's Delight."

"Sounds ominous." Rhoren walked over to the window. Even though the sky was a haze of rain, the heavy, dark gray clouds cast their shadow over the city.

"I hope the boy's father made it in safely." Helena looked over her shoulder toward the window. "I'd hate for anybody to be caught in that."

Thunder rumbled again, and Jinx hid under Helena's chair.

Kallum joined Rhoren at the window. "I hope James has enough sense to stay home with his sister."

"He's a smart kid." Rhoren grabbed a mop to busy himself from needless worry, but the Crookshank family stayed on his mind.

James didn't show for work, which both Rhoren and Kallum took as a good sign. Not that they needed him, because no one else ventured into the bar for the rest of the evening. Rain continued to pelt the streets of Eastborne, washing away any trace of the Storm Festival in the process.

After breaking down the bar for the evening, Kallum gathered his things. He hovered near the window as lightning flashed and rain whipped through the streets like sheets in the wind.

Rhoren found himself entranced by the storm's tenacity. He'd witnessed thundersnow and blizzards so dense that his hand disappeared if he reached his arm out, but he'd never seen rain do this. "You're welcome to stay here until the storm blows over."

Kallum let out a sigh of relief. "Thank the gods. I was afraid I might blow away trekking home."

"Who knows what will happen if that luxurious beard of yours gets wet?" Rhoren grinned. "You can have my bed. I'll take the couch."

"Nonsense." Kallum frowned, stroking his beard as if imagining it rain-soaked. "I'll take the couch. Keeping me out of the storm is generous enough."

Soon after, the two sat around the warmth of the fire, sharing a bottle of dwarven red wine as thunder rumbled in the distance. The crackle of burning logs and dull glow of the flames paired perfectly with the dry wine as the two talked of storms they had endured.

The hidden entrance swung open with a soft click, and

the spirit fox joined them. She always seemed to know when it was safe to come out, and soon, she and Jinx lay in front of the hearth, basking in its warmth.

By the time the bottle was empty, Rhoren's eyes hung heavy.

He stumbled to his feet. "Sweet dreams. I'll see you in the morning."

The bed welcomed him like an old friend, and once tucked away, the patter of rain played a soothing lullaby as the storm continued to roll in.

Rhoren woke to the sound of snarling. The spirit fox stood at the end of the bed, her hackles raised as she stared at the closed door to the balcony. The guttural growl continued to pour from the mythical beast as her lips pulled back around her teeth.

Downstairs, Jinx mirrored the fox with his own deep growls that carried up the stairwell. Rhoren wiped the sleep from his eyes and sat up, wondering what could have them both in a fit at this hour. Lightning struck outside the window, igniting the rain in a silver flash. The resounding thunder shook the building, and the hair on Rhoren's neck stood on end.

The fox's three tails hung low, tucked between her legs as she continued to voice her displeasure at something outside. Rhoren petted her on the nape as he crawled out of bed, but she remained focused on the door.

He approached the door with the finesse of a mouse, searching for some would-be intruder on the balcony, but he found it empty.

As he stared at the raging storm, a bolt of lightning tore through the night, crashing against the docks and igniting the harbor. One of the ships burst into flames, and in that moment of flashing light, Rhoren saw devastation.

Wreckage littered the bay. Masts lay strewn upon the pier along with the debris of battered ships no longer recognizable.

And then something moved in the darkness. A large tentacle reached up from the depths of the sea, clinging to the dock. A second tentacle emerged as a dark monstrosity made landfall, tearing through anything that stood in its path.

Kallum called from below, but Rhoren's pounding heart thundered above all.

A streak of purple cut through the night, exploding against the monster. A moment later, fireballs fizzled against its skin. Lightning arced through the air, conjured from someone on the ground.

Mages.

Whatever this monster was, the mages were trying to fight it off.

The city bells rang, and their deep bellow battled against the thunder. Rhoren opened the door and rain misted inside.

"Kraken!" The voice of a city crier carried through the night as a cloaked man shouted from the corner. "Kraken attack on the harbor."

A cold weight settled in Rhoren's stomach as the bells continued to toll. His vision darkened at the edges and ringing filled his ears.

Not again.

A firm hand gripped him on the arm, pulling him from his thoughts.

"What's happening?" Kallum squeezed harder to get Rhoren's attention. "Do you think there's actually a kraken?"

Rhoren tried to speak, but the words caught in his throat. A rainbow of magic continued to spark down by the pier, but the kraken—if that's what it was—had already climbed out of the sea. Rhoren raised a hand, pointing at the monster the size of a house.

"Gods be damned..." Kallum's voice faded into the ether.

"James," Rhoren croaked. "Cindy..."

His eyes locked onto the creature that moved unimpeded as magical attacks continued to assault it. It was like watching a child try to tear down a mountain. If this thing was a kraken, then it had a magically-resistant hide similar to a behemoth. The mages' attacks would be useless.

Rhoren grabbed his cloak and headed downstairs. Kallum protested behind him, but Rhoren didn't care. He'd sworn to defend the realm, to defend James and Cindy, and he would die before he broke that oath.

He pulled the front door open, and Kallum grabbed him by the arm.

"Wait! Rhoren, what are you doing?" There was pain and confusion in the man's eyes. "There's nothing you can do. You could barely function after your trek through the catacombs. How do you expect to fight a kraken?"

Rhoren jerked his arm free and set his shoulders with determination as he stared into the endless blue of

Kallum's eyes. A future of possibilities hid within their depths. A future he may never see.

He cradled Kallum's cheeks in shaking palms and pulled the man toward him. When their lips touched, the warmth pushed back the dread of what awaited.

Rhoren pressed his forehead to Kallum's and closed his eyes. "I don't know what I can do, but I have to try."

33. A CITY UNDER SIEGE

Rhoren sprinted toward the docks as rain pelted against his woolen cloak and thunder rumbled in his bones. Fires burned down by the harbor like fireflies on a foggy night. Lightning flashed sporadically, revealing snippets of the carnage below.

The flicker of magical attacks moved across the river as the kraken changed course toward the Lower District. Toward James and Cindy.

The brilliant display of power vanished behind buildings as he passed through the lower levels of the city. Rhoren pushed himself to go faster, ignoring the burn within his lungs as his body begged for air. The cool rain against his face turned his skin to gooseflesh, but the memory of Kallum's kiss still burned on his lips. He turned that fire to fuel and ran harder.

Another bolt of lightning revealed the growing destruction. Shattered masts buoyed at sea next to the floundering hulls of once-great ships, and tattered sails whipped like strands of silk in the night.

The rainy streets were no longer empty as hordes of people rushed past him, soaked to the bone in their night-clothes as they searched for higher ground and the hope of safety.

Rhoren's heart pounded in his ears, drowning out the rain and terrified screams. A man bumped into him, and Rhoren fell to the ground. For a moment, he was no longer in Eastborne. He was back in Hollowton at six years old.

He sat around a crackling fire watching the embers shoot into the air and turn to ash. Frost coated the nearby window, concealing a snowy landscape on the other side. At the table, his mother made fireweed tea. She smiled across the table at Rhoren's father as he whittled a piece of wood into the shape of a wolf.

Though his father had said it wasn't for Rhoren, the elf's mischievous smile told him it would be a part of his collection soon.

A loud roar from outside made his father pause, and a moment later the sound of splintering wood tore through their peaceful evening like an avalanche. Panicked screams arose from outside, and Rhoren's father ran across the room. He wiped away the fog of the street-facing window and peered into the village. People ran by, constantly looking over their shoulders.

Another roar caused his mother to knock over the tea kettle, and the minty-citrus aroma of fireweed tea filled their small home.

Outside, there was more destruction. More screams.

Rhoren's father grabbed their cloaks and opened the door without a word.

"What's happening?" Rhoren asked.

His father wrapped a hand around each of his small arms and squeezed. "We have to go."

The air was crisp against his cheeks as he followed his father into the night. The glow of the moon reflected off the snow, and there was no darkness. Nowhere to hide.

People rushed past, running from some unseen terror. Fear swelled inside Rhoren even though he didn't know the cause. His short legs trudged through the snow, and when a roar rang out, unimpeded by the four walls of their small home, he froze in place. His mother took hold of his arm, ushering him forward. He tried to follow, but his legs buckled, and he fell into the snow.

Rhoren closed his eyes, blocking out what came next. When he opened them, he was once again in the crowded streets of Eastborne as a monster lay siege to the city.

He stood and continued to fight his way through the crowd toward James and Cindy.

By the time he crossed the bridge, the streets were sparse. Buildings lay in ruin from where the kraken had passed through, but the sounds of its rampage could be heard nearby. He followed the trail of devastation as it led in the direction of the Crookshank home.

His heart sank when he discovered the balcony where Ol' Bessy had yelled at him was gone, along with the entire block. The homes of those who had the least were now nothing more than rubble. The monster had shifted its path before reaching the Crookshank house, but it was empty all the same.

He prayed that James had the wherewithal to get as far away from the attack as possible.

Rhoren passed city guards as they escorted the injured to safety, and he found the monstrous creature propelling itself on large tentacles toward the Warehouse District. The tentacles ripped through stone and wood, tearing houses and storefronts apart like they were made of gingerbread.

When Rhoren finally set eyes upon the monster, it was even more fearsome than he'd imagined. Every part of his being told him to run, but he stood firm. The kraken's head was the size of a carriage, with large purple eyes that burned red within their depths. Beneath its sinister eyes, a silver beak snapped at the air, surrounded by a half-dozen barbels that thrashed about. Massive tentacles held the kraken upright, each one as thick as a black oak and covered in barbs, while the suctions on the underside gripped with serrated edges.

It was a being born of nightmares, and a half-dozen mages surrounded the monster as they tried to bring it down. They kept their distance as they attacked it from all angles, but the spells exploding against its shimmering skin had little effect.

The kraken rose on its tentacles, taller than any of the surrounding buildings. Its beak opened, and the barbels fluttered as a shrill cry ripped through the night.

Rhoren would not have blamed the mages for faltering in that moment, but they answered the challenge. One of the mages' arms glowed as she reached toward the river. Water rose and formed a tidal wave that crashed down on the kraken. The monster smashed into a building, destroying two walls as it crushed the structure with its weight. Ice encased the kraken and for a moment, it was nothing more than a crystalline statue. The ice shattered from its massive frame just as lightning shot from the hands of a third mage, followed by a stream of fire from another. The ground tore apart and closed around one of the kraken's arms.

But the attacks only made it angrier. The kraken ripped its arm free, leaving a crater in the street as it used the rock encasing its tentacle like a bludgeon to level two more buildings before the rock crumbled from its limb.

The mages shouted at one another, but Rhoren was too far away to make sense of it. He needed to get closer.

He passed through several alleys as he tried to flank the mages. There was a sizzle of magical energy just before the ground shook and debris rained from above. Rhoren clung to the wall until it passed. He ran through another alley before stopping in front of a large wall.

Icy dread settled on his shoulders. This was the wall surrounding the alchemy colony. If the kraken passed through, there was no telling the damage it might cause.

He followed the perimeter until the kraken became visible again. The mages still kept themselves out of its reach, but they had done little to slow it down.

Rhoren approached with caution, and when he was close enough for them to hear, he shouted, "We can't let it pass through the colony."

"Get out of here!" The fire mage's eyes raged like an inferno. "You're going to get yourself killed."

The mage had no idea how true his words were.

"You can't stop it on your own." Rhoren's words were so matter-of-fact that the fire faded from the mage's eyes.

He took in Rhoren's appearance, frowning when he noticed the emblem of the Northern Guard on his cloak. "Who are you?"

That was the question, wasn't it? The one Rhoren had

been searching for all his life. And it seemed that he'd found the answer in the unlikeliest of places.

"I am Rhoren Balsalor, son of Dhorian Balsalor... though some call me Bloodbane."

Recognition dawned on the mage's face, and there was grim acknowledgment as he stepped aside.

Rhoren removed his cloak and tossed it to the ground. Rain soaked through his shirt in an instant, and a chill passed through his body. *Good, because this is going to burn like hell.*

The kraken shrieked its challenge, halfway perched on a crumbling building, and the other mages fell back. Rhoren stepped to the forefront and closed his eyes.

He activated his blood sense, and his veins unleashed a scream that rivaled the kraken's. The hearts of the six mages beat frantically, all except the ice mage whose heart pulsed with the rhythm of a hibernating bear. One heart thundered above them all with a slow pounding that shook Rhoren as he focused on it. It was an angry heartbeat that took up the entirety of his mind's eye, violent in its intensity.

Rhoren focused on the monster's heart and squeezed. His veins burned with white-hot fervor as they threatened to unravel from his power. He held the monster in place, but for the first time in his life, he felt an authority that matched his own. He applied pressure, and the heart pushed back. He pressed down on the kraken's life force with everything he had, but still, it didn't fold.

Stars flashed across the blackness of the void, and his grip faltered. A shrill cry cut through the night, through the pain, and he realized that it was his own voice calling for help.

He breathed in the cool night air, and the stars burnt out. The kraken's heart pulsed angrily in his mind's eye as he wrestled for control.

His grip faltered as a wave of rage pressed against him, but then a swirl of energy appeared across the void as trails of wispy blue light flowed into the darkness in the shape of a fox. *She watches. Always watching.* The three tails swished, and a calming sensation filled the void.

Rhoren gathered himself and refocused his efforts. If he didn't stop the kraken right here and now, he would lose everything he'd built, everything he loved. Everything.

He refused to let that happen. He squeezed around the monster's heart until his skin burned and his bones felt like they had turned to dust. Fire raged within his mind and his heart, and he'd gladly take the pain if it meant saving the ones he loved.

He fought until his body turned cold, and everything faded to black.

34. ALL FOR SOMETHING

Bright light seeped through the darkness, and Rhoren wondered if this was what death felt like. Birds chirped, and a warm breeze passed over him. Followed by pain.

So much pain.

His eyes squinted open, and the blur of the city shrouded his vision. His body burned from head to toe. If this was death, then he was certainly in one hell or another. A man with broad shoulders and shaggy black hair held the arms of the cart as it rolled along. Every bump was agony. Rhoren tried to fight through the pain and sit up, but the world spun. He let his head fall. He closed his eyes and drifted back to the darkness.

Rhoren drifted in and out of consciousness until time held no meaning. It could have been hours, days, or weeks for all he knew.

Fragments of scenes played out before him, speckling his slumber and following him into his dreams. He lay in bed under Kallum's watchful gaze as the man held his hand. A cleric visited. Jinx curled upon his chest, purring contentedly. A cold nose pressed against him as the spirit fox nudged his cheek. Concerned looks as Cindy and James sat on each side of him.

His thoughts were dull, and he could only watch the images unfold. There was no energy to ponder their significance.

When the shroud finally lifted, Rhoren found Kallum asleep in a chair beside the bed. Both Jinx and the spirit fox lay curled around his feet. He groaned as he pushed himself to a sitting position, his body aching with every movement.

Jinx meowed and nuzzled closer to Rhoren.

Kallum stirred at the noise, and his eyes went wide when he noticed that Rhoren was awake. He rushed over, sitting on the edge of the bed and cradling Rhoren's face in his palms. "You stupid, stupid elf. Thank the gods you survived."

Rhoren wrapped his hands around Kallum's. "How long was I out?"

"Three days." He sighed, releasing his hold. "The longest three days of my life."

"I'm sorry." Rhoren looked past Kallum to the window, where blue skies hid any memory of the previous storm.

Kallum shook his head. "You don't owe me an apology. You saved the city. All of Eastborne is in your debt."

Rhoren tried to recall his fight with the kraken, but much of it still blurred together. "What happened?"

"You killed a kraken, Rhor. To hear the mages tell it, it was like you were empowered by the gods themselves.

The moment it fell, the storm cleared for miles in every direction."

Rhoren grimaced. "Everyone knows I'm a blood mage now?"

Kallum nodded.

"I'm sorry." His face fell with a sigh. "Maybe Timofey will take you back at the Seaside Inn."

"What are you talking about?" Kallum's brow furrowed so deep, his eyes almost disappeared.

"Nobody is going to want to come to a bar owned by a blood mage."

"I wouldn't be so sure about that. Here, let me show you something." Kallum offered his arm to Rhoren and helped the elf out of bed.

Slowly, they walked over to the stairs, where chatter could be heard below. Jinx darted in front of them, and the noise faded. One step at a time, Kallum helped Rhoren down the stairwell.

He entered into a bar full of people. They sat in silence, every eye focused on him. There was a shuffle of feet as Cindy ran over and wrapped her arms around him, followed by James. His aches renewed with fresh life, but he'd die before he pushed the two of them away. Then, the entire bar stood and clapped as Rhoren placed an arm around both children.

He recognized many familiar faces. Helena, Hewelet, Titus and his wife, Jesper, Ametrine, Darvish Goldhammer, Timofey, and many more. There were no cocktails, but wine glasses and beer mugs covered the tables, and a plate of coins sat on the bar next to several uncorked bottles.

Rhoren turned to Kallum. "What is this?"

"These are your friends, Rhoren. And they are here if you need anything."

Tomas walked over and tapped his children on their shoulders. "That's enough of that. Give Rhoren some space." He nodded to Rhoren. "Kallum told me why you were down there to begin with." Tears welled up in the man's eyes, threatening to run down his freckled cheeks. "Thank you."

Before anyone else had a chance to come over, Kallum raised a hand to gather their attention. "Alright, alright. The elf just killed a kraken, for gods' sakes. Let him have a seat first."

Helena stood from her chair by the fire and offered a kind smile. "You can sit here, Rhoren."

"Nonsense." Jesper stood from the chair beside her. "Take mine. I'll play some music."

Rhoren passed by Jesper as he made his way to the hearth. The two stopped, and Rhoren steadied himself on the young man's powerful frame.

"You brought me back here." It wasn't a question as he recalled the memory of moving by cart through the city.

"I did." Jesper brushed a strand of black hair from his brow. "Once the storm cleared and Kallum told us what happened, we came down to find you. The procession that followed us through the city on our return would have put the festival to shame." He placed a hand gently on Rhoren's shoulder. "I saw the body of the kraken. I don't know how you did it."

"That makes two of us." Rhoren smiled as he looked around the room. "But I know *why* I did it."

Rhoren took a seat in the oversized chair by the fire,

while Jesper stepped onto the stage. He didn't sing but simply strummed his lute in a soothing melody.

Kallum sat next to Rhoren on the arm of the chair, and their fingers interlocked. As much as he ached, Rhoren found that the pain was the least of his concerns. Somehow, he'd found his people far away from everything he'd ever known, and in the end, the one thing that had defined him for so long didn't seem to matter much at all.

EPILOGUE: AN OLD FRIEND

Five Months Later.

Rhoren sliced lemons behind the bar in the early morning as he prepped for the day. His mind wandered as he worked, ruminating on all the tasks that still awaited. Jinx sat on the counter, watching the motion of the knife as it rose and fell.

The door opened, and Rhoren spoke without looking up. "Sorry, but we don't open for a few hours."

"Is that how you treat an old friend?"

Rhoren looked up to find a short, stout dwarf standing in the doorway.

He wore the robes of a cleric and smiled beneath his braided black beard. "Bloodbane."

Rhoren ran around the bar, embracing the dwarf with a firm hug. "Charence! What in the hells are you doing here?"

Charence patted Rhoren on the back. "Word of your exploits has traveled far and wide. Some are calling you Bloodbane Krakenkiller."

"That's a mouthful if I've ever heard one." He motioned toward the bar. "Come. Have a seat. Let me get you a drink."

Charence nodded approvingly. "I'm glad you took some of my advice to heart. You know, I half-expected to find you dead by the time I arrived."

"Sorry to disappoint." Rhoren smirked.

"How I've missed your humor."

The two continued to talk as if no time had passed while Rhoren made Charence a drink.

"How are you feeling?" the cleric asked.

Rhoren muddled lime in the bottom of the glass. "Better now. It took weeks before I could move around properly, but Timofey, gods bless him, he let his bartenders pick up extra shifts here until I came around. You wouldn't believe how good almost dying can be for business."

"Oh, I believe it." Charence chuckled. "I'm glad you've found some purpose in your life."

"I've found more than that." Rhoren grinned.

"Really?" His brows arched. "Has the brooding Blood-bane finally found room for another in that cold, cramped heart?"

Rhoren blushed. "Something like that."

"That's good. You've sacrificed enough."

Rhoren leaned against the bar. "So what brings you this far south?"

"You mean besides seeing an old friend?" When Rhoren didn't answer, he continued. "You know the nature of my business. When a kraken makes landfall for the first time in five hundred years, it's my job to investigate."

Rhoren frowned as his gaze shifted to the window, where the morning sun shined through. "You think there's more to it?"

"I certainly hope not. But we don't survive on hopes and prayers."

"Is that the official position of the Order of Clerics?" Rhoren's lips trembled as he tried to hold back his grin.

Charence rolled his eyes when the door opened again.

"We're clo— Oh, it's you."

"Rhoren, by the gods, I am wounded. To be met with such words." Jesper placed a hand over his heart. "I've been working on a new song to play tonight. I wanted to rehearse for a bit, if that's okay."

"That's fine. I'm just chatting with an old friend."

While Jesper tuned his lute, Charence changed the subject to talk of the city, the bar, and everything Rhoren had made of himself in Eastborne. Jinx jumped onto the bar, interested in the clasp that dangled from the dwarf's beard.

After a long while of playing and humming, Jesper cleared his throat. "I call this one *The Bar and the Blood Mage.*"

To read the bonus epilogue Flint & Embers, *head over to*
SLRowland.com/cursed

DOWNLOAD THE RECIPES OF
CURSED COCKTAILS

Sign up for S.L. Rowland's News-letter and receive *Devilish Drinks: A Recipe Guide to the Novel Cursed Cocktails.*

Click here to sign up!
Or visit SLRowland.com

ACKNOWLEDGMENTS

Thank you for reading *Cursed Cocktails*! Please rate, review, and spread the love on social media using the hashtag #cursedcocktails. Word of mouth is the best way to help indie authors like myself.

Although writing is often a solitary profession, stories are very rarely created in a vacuum. I should first acknowledge that this story wouldn't exist without Travis Baldree. I was reading *Legends & Lattes* when the idea for Rhoren first entered my mind. Over the months that followed, Rhoren's story continued to unfold, and the world of Aedrea grew into what it is today.

My good friend Scotty Heyden was instrumental in helping me make sense of the world in those early days, asking the hard questions, and he even helped create an early draft of the map of Aedrea.

Sean Flint was an invaluable resource for all things spirit-related, and helped with the cocktail selection that inspired the drinks of *Cursed Cocktails*.

Once again, Cindy Koepp offered her feedback on the earliest of drafts, and my betas readers took it one step further. Thank you to Cindy, Loren Foster, Sami Taylor,

Sean Flint, Paul Tuson, Greg Trotti, and Tom Nemes for your feedback and attention to detail.

Thank you to Caroline for the constant support in times of elation, productivity, utter laziness, and bouts of self-doubt. You bring peace to the chaos.

I would also like to thank all of my patrons on Patreon:

Platinum Tier: Joel Southard

Gold Tier: Michael Percell and Robert Schaefer

Silver Tier: Nicholas Kelly and Sami Taylor

Bronze Tier: Cindy Koepp, Rachael Osterhout, Rickie Brookes, Roxanne Baechler-Gill, and Eric Sprague

If you'd like to find more cozy fantasy reads, stop by the Cozy Fantasy Subreddit

ABOUT THE AUTHOR

S.L. Rowland is a wanderer. Whether that's getting lost in the woods or road-tripping coast to coast with his Shiba Inu, Lawson, he goes where the wind blows. When not writing, he enjoys hiking, reading, weightlifting, playing video games, and having his heart broken by various Atlanta sports teams.

Find out more at https://linktr.ee/SLRowland

SLRowland.com

Patreon-For signed paperbacks, advanced chapters, exclusive short stories, art, merch, and more. This is a great way to show your support between releases.

Newsletter: For updates on new releases and all things Pangea Online related! Click the link at the end of the book to download *Path to Villainy* for free.

Email: slrowlandauthor@gmail.com

ALSO BY S.L. ROWLAND

Tales of Aedrea

Cursed Cocktails

Sword & Thistle

Pangea Online

Pangea Online: Death and Axes

Pangea Online 2: Magic and Mayhem

Pangea Online 3: Vials and Tribulations

Sentenced to Troll

Sentenced to Troll

Sentenced to Troll 2

Sentenced to Troll 3

Sentenced to Troll 4

Sentenced to Troll 5

Path to Villainy: An NPC Kobold's Tale

Collected Editions

Pangea Online: The Complete Trilogy

Sentenced to Troll Compendium: Books 1-3

Printed in Great Britain
by Amazon

44769114R10158